T

The Book of the Virgins

Il Libro delle Vergini

Gabriele D'Annunzio

Translated by J.G. Nichols

ET REMOTISSIMA PROPE

100 PAGES

100 PAGES
Published by Hesperus Press Limited
4 Rickett Street, London SW6 1RU
www.hesperuspress.com

First published in Italian as *Il Libro delle Vergini* in 1884;
© Arnoldo Mondadori Editore, S.p.A., Milano, 1927
This translation first published by Hesperus Press Limited, 2003

Introduction and English language translation © J.G. Nichols, 2003
Foreword © Tim Parks, 2003

Designed and typeset by Fraser Muggeridge
Printed in the United Arab Emirates by Oriental Press

ISBN: 1-84391-052-7

CONTENTS

Nothing drives a narrative better than repression. When we hear in Shakespeare's *Measure for Measure* of Angelo's ruthless purity we are already determined that it be corrupted. This man must be humiliated by lust. Nothing else will satisfy us. When we see a story entitled *The Virgins*, we are tensed for the deflowering. All the stories in this book are essentially tales of awakening, but not the kind that brings enlightenment. Rather, the lucid mind is overwhelmed by a compulsion before which every rule and taboo is suddenly obsolete. A river, usually no more than a distant murmur, has broken its banks. The everyday world is submerged in sensuality, utterly sexualised. Sensory perceptions fantastically enhanced, the will drowns in a flood of feeling.

Transgression is usually taken as a hallmark of vocation in a writer. The poet's sins assure us that he is the real thing. Not so with D'Annunzio. On the rare occasions when he does nudge his way into the Anglo-Saxon consciousness, it is always for the wrong reasons. He is the rabid nationalist who urged Italy to join the First World War. He is the egocentric adventurer whose mad volunteers, in defiance of international law, occupied Fiume on the north Adriatic coast in 1919. He preached the superman (along with Carlyle and Nietzsche and Shaw), and was friends with Mussolini. Even his sexual trespasses win him little credit. There is something farcical about the ageing man who orders the bells of his villa to be rung whenever he achieves orgasm with the umpteenth mistress. An old alliance between piety and caution, between Church and socialism – something we have recently learnt to call political correctness – has written off D'Annunzio as a monomaniac. His style, they tell us, is excessive, verbose. They don't want us to open his books. I was kept away for years.

A dozen pages of *The Virgins* will dispel these prejudices. D'Annunzio surprises us. One of two spinster sisters is dying of typhus. These young women have given up their lives to God and to the community, teaching catechism and basic grammar to young children in their home. The priest arrives to give extreme unction. The host is placed on a tongue dark with blood and mucus. The evocation of a suffocatingly religious, peasant atmosphere, of a mortal sickness in all its ugliness, stench and mental stupor, is dense and marvellously paced. Sentence by sentence, we are waiting for the woman to die, begging for it to be over.

Giuliana doesn't die, and D'Annunzio is not just another practitioner of nineteenth-century social realism. Far from cancelling out the old Adam and ushering another soul through the pearly gates, the last rites appear to have returned Giuliana to a state before the Fall. She is back from the dead and intensely sensitive to the mystery of her healing body, as if experiencing the throes of a second puberty. A subtle symbolism informs the plot but, as with Hardy's or Lawrence's finest work, it springs naturally from the world we know, offering but never imposing a possible order. In the shameless hunger of first convalescence, Giuliana searches the house for food while her sister is away at mass. She finds an old apple and bites deep to the seeds. A heady, rosy perfume is released. Giuliana laughs, as anyone returning to health would laugh, and laughter is of the devil. She finds a mirror, studies her face, then, more boldly, her naked body. All at once we have a fiercely sexed young woman, adult and virgin, dangerously innocent, living and sleeping beside a sister, who, in her repressive religious devotion, seems 'the corpse of a martyr'. It is Camilla who is dead. Not Giuliana.

At last the convalescent goes to the window and draws back the curtain. The smell of fresh bread drifts up seductively from the bakery below, the blast of the trumpet sounds the hours from the nearby barracks where the soldiers whistle to the passing girls. The reader is gripped by a powerful sense that something tremendous is about to happen.

Place is important. Pescara is at the same height as Rome on the Italian peninsula, but on the opposite coast, the Adriatic. Busy, provincial, backward, the town forms a ribbon of chaotic life between coastal pinewoods and rugged hills that rise steeply to the high plateaux of the Abruzzi mountains. Winter rains and snow fill the streets with rushing water. Spring is an explosion of rich smells. The violent summer sun glares off white limestone, tortures the dark vegetation, glitters on the sea. Himself in love with extremity, D'Annunzio has an uncanny ability to capture every manifestation of climate and landscape, bucolic or grotesque, threatening or lush. Far from being superfluous, his descriptions set in motion the brooding drama of a huge and inexorable natural process, against which the moral pretensions of religion and society are increasingly felt to be meaningless. In one of these stories a bleeding woman stumbles into a house to collapse and die, while a solitary, blind old man taps uncomprehending about the corpse with his stick. Nothing could better express D'Annunzio's sense of the fatal elusiveness of life and death to rational enquiry.

Altered states of mind, sickness, passion, delirium are the norm in these stories. A woman and her husband's brother are pampering her young daughter in the presence of his elderly mother. Adult fingers meet by chance in the child's thick blond hair; unplanned and unwanted, a passion begins that sweeps away the claims of parenthood, the duties of son to dying mother. 'Aren't you afraid of enchantments?' one character asks in another story. You should be, is D'Annunzio's answer. It is this apprehension of the subjection of the mind to the magic of the world, or to organic processes, if you like, coupled with a conviction that established prescriptions for good behaviour are quite obsolete, that will ultimately lead D'Annunzio to his cult of the superman, the figure whose will is so strong that he can stamp new patterns of value on life. That dangerous figure is absent from these stories, which present us rather with life's victims, yet latent all the same, and understandable.

Teaching proper Italian to their infant pupils, the two virgin sisters broke up the language into its constituent parts – *la, le, li, lo, lu*, they made the children repeat, *nar, ner, nir, nor, nur...* Returning to new life after her terrible illness, Giuliana listens to her sister repeating these formulae – *ram, rem, rim, rom, rum* – and finds them intolerable. She sobs and beats her fists on the pillow. These rigid patterns and divisions are death to those truly alive. The moment can be considered emblematic of the birth of Modernism. From now on, everything is to be mixed and fizzing with life: male and female, ugly and beautiful, sacred and profane, poetry and prose, above all good and evil. The most unexpected words appear together, sacred images disclose all their eroticism, erotic gestures are made in complete innocence. Decades before their day, this is the world of Lawrence and Joyce.

– *Tim Parks, 2003*

In his lifetime Gabriele D'Annunzio was famous, celebrated, notorious, infamous – it is difficult to find the right word to indicate the reactions to him and his work – but for reasons which were often more to do with his life than his writing. This was, because of the language barrier, particularly the case outside Italy. For instance, in England he was, during the First World War, not only well known but respected. A sufficient reason for this was his influence in bringing Italy into the war (on the right side of course!). But it is doubtful if he has ever been much read in England. That might not matter so much if his life had been more than superficially admirable. His most recent biographer, John Woodhouse, speaks of the difficulty of finding one instance in D'Annunzio's longish life where he shows true sympathy for anyone else. The Italians have a word for his guiding principle – *egolatria*, the worship of oneself, which could provide us with a useful word in English, 'egolatry', a stage beyond narcissism. That is not the greatest of our difficulties in accepting him: the worship of power, the cult of the ruthless and amoral individual, the fascism in short, is not to most people's taste nowadays. He was a fascist *avant la lettre*, and Mussolini turned to him for tips. In retrospect, the strident self-publicising for which Guido Gozzano mocked him seems a comparatively venial fault:

> *The laurel-crown*
> *these days is kept for him who blossoms out*
> *on hearing trumpets blown (he blows his own),*
> *who hogs the limelight, who's a charlatan*
> *never quite happy till he's talked about...*
> (*La Signorina Felicita*)

The cover of the first edition of *The Book of the Virgins* was described even by D'Annunzio himself as obscene. And yet his apparent objection was very probably a way of drawing attention to a good selling point. As so often in discussing D'Annunzio, we are drawn to features which have no necessary connection with the writing itself.

At times the work can repel too. The first of the stories here, 'The

Virgins', is described by Woodhouse as 'scurrilous'. He uses the word in the middle of a discussion of the use of real, easily identifiable people as models for the 'fictional' characters. The word that occurs to me is simply 'unpleasant': the passive suffering and degradation of a woman who is at the mercy of physical changes she cannot control is not tragic, but pathetic, and its description is not exhilarating in any way except – and this is the crunch – for the occasional grace and appositeness of the style.

It is time, I think, to separate the man from the work, to push our knowledge of the numerous discarded mistresses, the ridiculous attack on Fiume, the unremitting self-glorification, to the back of our minds, and concentrate on the words on the page, which can be exhilarating.

Keats famously expressed his longing for a life of sensation, rather than thought. The characters in these stories may be said to live the kind of life that Keats desired, although not always with the enjoyment he had in mind. There is very little direct speech in these stories, and even less introspection on the part of the protagonists: it is their sensations that are dwelt upon. The first story, 'The Virgins', even reads at times rather like a doctor's case-notes. This can give a not unpleasing objectivity to the accounts, a 'realism', in that the writer's feelings do not seem to be involved. The same result comes from the frequent, and frequently effective, descriptions of outward things. Sometimes these descriptions are of clothing, and then they read less like a doctor's case-notes and very much like a fashion editor's column. The point is not merely that D'Annunzio was a man for whom the external world mattered, perhaps at times too much, but that he used it to indicate, without mawkishness, states of mind. We are in the presence of our old friend the 'objective correlative', although – to do him justice – D'Annunzio would have had no truck with such an unappealing expression, or even with the critical activity behind it.

To take just three examples from the first story:

After the brief description of the arrival of the priest with the viaticum at the start, everything happens indoors in the claustrophobic atmosphere of the virgins' home. Then Giuliana's recovery from her illness comes alive to us in the description of the scene in the street outside:

'There were certain clear, cold evenings when the whole region of Pescara was peopled with sailors and filled with the sound of bagpipes.'

A fresh world breaks in, and with it fresh sensations. Later, as religion gives way to eroticism, we are told that:

'…the aphrodisiacal light of the moon was encircled with all the epithets which make the Holy Spirit radiant…'

The close connection between religious feeling and erotic feeling, implicit in the action of this story, is not an aperçu of D'Annunzio's – it is indeed a literary and artistic commonplace (although not always overtly recognised) and responsible for much of the attraction of both forms of activity: here its ramifications are explored. The terrible guilt which Giuliana feels near the end of the story is conveyed, better than it could be by any words of such an unselfconscious person as she is, once again by an external description:

'A magnificent red cloud stood over the buildings, like that cloud perhaps which poured fire and brimstone down on the wickedness of Sodom.'

Similarly, in the second story here, Galatea's liking for the over-shadowed and rank garden is not simply the filling-in of little details expected of a novelist, but an appropriate symbol of the life she leads. The description may be intrusive in the fondness with which it dwells on the repellent details, but it is not obtrusive as a piece of symbolism, but simply right.

D'Annunzio was never noted for his sense of humour, but there are touches in this book of a self-awareness in the writing which is very close to humour. When, in the story 'In Lanciotto's Absence', Francesca and Gustavo come to the point of acknowledging their love, we are told:

'It is something which usually happens in any riding-expedition involving two people, in novels and in real life.'

Then there is a later passage:

'At that moment the moon rose slowly through the trees, chaste and silvery, according to custom…'

There is here a sudden standing back from the situation described, foreshadowing even the reaction against D'Annunzianism which we associate most closely with Guido Gozzano, one of whose protagonists

> …*lingered by the cemetery gate*
> *as people do in books of poetry.*
> (*La Signorina Felicita*)

This book is not vintage D'Annunzio: after all, he was only twenty-one when it was published. But there is evidence in it of the direction his writing would take, and there are many compelling passages. If, as those last two passages of his that are quoted indicate, he was at times too much the aesthete, more interested in books than people, then that surely is a fault to be pardoned by people who read books.

– J. G. Nichols, 2003

Note on the Text:
The current text is based on Gabriele D'Annunzio: *Il Libro delle Vergini*, Mondadori (1980). The passages in the Introduction quoted from Guido Gozzano are from *Guido Gozzano. The Colloquies and selected letters*, translated by J.G. Nichols (Carcanet, 1987).

The Virgins

The viaticum came out of the church at midday. The first flakes of snow were on all the streets, and snow covered all the houses. But up in the sky large islands of blue appeared between the snow clouds, spread slowly above the Brina Palace, and shone out in the direction of the Bandiera. And in the white air, upon the white land, there suddenly and miraculously appeared the comforting sun.

The viaticum was going to Giuliana's house. People stopped to watch the priest passing, as he proceeded bareheaded, wearing a violet stole, beneath the broad scarlet umbrella, in the midst of burning lamps carried by the altar-boys. The bell was ringing out clearly – an accompaniment to the psalms murmured by the priest. Stray dogs moved out of the way into the alleys at the side of the road. Mazzanti stopped piling up the snow at the corner of the square and bared his bald head and bowed. At that moment from Flajano's oven the warm, wholesome smell of newly baked bread spread through the air, a smell to tickle the palate.

Those who were present in the sick woman's house heard the bell, and heard the new arrivals coming up the stairs. Giuliana was lying on her back in bed, overcome by the fever, inert and torpid, her rapid breathing interrupted by occasional wheezing. On the whiteness of the pillow rested her almost hairless head, with her face practically sky-blue, her eyelids half closed upon her viscid eyes, and her nostrils looking as though they were blackened by smoke. Her fleshless hands made tiny unconscious movements, vague attempts to take hold of something in the void, sudden strange signs which communicated a feeling of terror to those who were standing by; at times there were muscular contractions in her pale arms, tendons jerking; at times an unintelligible stammering came from her lips, as if her words had become entangled in the soot that was on her tongue, in the sticky mucus on her gums.

There was in the room that tragic silence which always comes at the last hours, a silence in which the sick woman's breathing and her uncertain gestures and hoarse bursts of bronchial coughing took on a kind of funereal solemnity. Through the open windows pure air came in and the exhalations of illness went out. An intense white gleam was reflected off the snow covering the cornices and Corinthian capitals of the Portanova Arch; a crystalline efflorescence of icicles glittered with all the colours of the rainbow at the same height as the room. Inside it, the walls were hung with large brass holy medals and pictures of saints. Under glass a Madonna of Loreto could be seen, with her face, her breast, and her arms quite black like a barbarian idol, glorified by her golden dress on which half-moons were rising. In one corner a small white altar rose up, with an old ivory Jesus on a cross inlaid with mother-of-pearl, and with a pair of deep blue Castelli pots full of aromatic herbs.

Camilla, her sister and her only relative, who was very pale, was cleaning the invalid's blackish lips and encrusted teeth with a piece of linen soaked in vinegar. Don Vincenzo Bucci, the doctor, sat and looked at the silver knob of his fine walking stick, and the beautiful cornelians set into the rings on his fingers, waiting. Teodora La Jece, a weaver who lived nearby, remained standing, in silence, concentrating on giving to her white, freckled face, her eyes as grey as lead, and her cruel mouth an expression of grief.

'*Pax huic domui*,'[1] said the priest as he entered. Don Gennaro Tierno appeared in the doorway, very tall and thin and angular, resting on enormous feet. Behind him came Rosa Catena, a woman who had made public profession of her immodesty in her salad days and was now saving her soul by attending the dying, washing their corpses, clothing them, and arranging them on the bier, without any pay.

In Giuliana's room they were now all on their knees, with their heads bent. The sick woman could not hear anything: her senses still lay in torpor. And the aspergillum was raised over her, shining in the air, sprinkling the bed.

'*Asperges me, domine, hyssopo, et mundabor…*'[2] But Giuliana did not feel the purifying waters that were washing her whiter than snow in the presence of her Lord.

Her feeble fingers were tugging at the covers in front of her, her lips were quivering, the words she could not produce were gurgling in her throat.

'*Exaudi nos, domine sancte…*'[3]

4

At that point a burst of weeping resounded through the Latin words, and Camilla hid her tear-streaked face on the edge of the bed. The doctor had approached and was holding Giuliana's wrist between his ringed fingers. He was trying to rouse her, prepare her to receive the Sacrament from the hands of the priest of Jesus Christ, make her put out her tongue for the host.

Giuliana babbled, gesticulated, still vaguely unconscious, while they were propping her up on her pillows. She must have felt the nerves of her ears tingling, disturbed perhaps by the cries, or perhaps by music. When she was sitting up, the livid redness of her face suddenly changed into a corpse-like pallor; the ice pack fell from her head onto the sheet.

'*Misereatur…*'[4]

At last she did put out her trembling tongue, crusted with a mixture of mucus and blackish blood, where the pure Host came to rest.

'*Ecce agnus Dei, ecce qui tollit peccata mundi…*'[5]

But she did not withdraw her tongue on its contact with the Host, because she did not know what she was doing: her stupefaction had not been disturbed by the light of the Eucharist. Camilla, her red eyes full of terror and grief, looked at that ashen face from which every sign of life was gradually ebbing away, that open mouth which looked like the mouth of someone who had been throttled. With all the solemnity of his ministry, the priest continued to pray slowly in Latin. All the others remained genuflecting, in the diffused glow created by the light of midday on the snow outside. A gust of wind brought the scent of warm bread and tickled the nerve-ends in the noses of the altar-boys.

'*Oremus…*'[6]

At the encouragement of the doctor, Giuliana closed her lips again. They laid her down on her back once more, because the priest was starting on the sacrament of extreme unction. From the kneeling altar-boys came the low sound of the antiphons of the penitential psalms.

'*Ne reminiscaris.*'[7]

Teodora La Jece gave a strangled sob from time to time, covering her face with her hands at the foot of the bed. Rosa Catena remained standing to one side, one half-closed eye flowing continually with a yellowish liquid, the other eye blind and white with leucoma, running a rosary through her fingers and muttering. And while the psalms were softly rising from the floor, that confused murmur was dominated by the sacred formula of the priest anointing with the sign of the cross the eyes, the ears, the nostrils, the mouth, the hands of the inert invalid.

'...*indulgeat tibi Dominus quidquid per gressum deliquisti. Amen.*'[8]

It was Camilla who uncovered her sister's feet. From under the covers appeared two yellow feet, scaly, their nails blue, loathsome to the touch like dead limbs. And Camilla's tears fell onto that dry skin, mixed with the consecrated oil.

'*Kyrie eleison. Christe eleison. Kyrie eleison. Pater noster...*'[9]

She who was anointed by the Lord was now left motionless, her eyes closed against the light, her knees raised, and her hands pressed between her thighs in that attitude so customary with sufferers from typhus. And the priest, once he had pressed the crucifix to her lips for the last time, and made the sign of the cross high in the middle of the room with his big hand, went out, followed by the altar-boys. In the room there still floated that faint odour of incense and wax which belongs to priestly garments. Outside, under the windows, Matteo Puriello was hammering away at the sole of a shoe and humming.

2

The symptoms of sickness slowly waned and things took a favourable turn. There now succeeded the fourth week, and the numb drowsiness was followed by a peaceful natural sleep, a lasting peace in which little by little all the perturbations of consciousness calmed down, and her senses became less troubled and she breathed more steadily. But a rasping cough broke out at times in the sick woman's breast, shaking her backbone; a grievous destruction of the skin and soft tissues at her elbows, her knees, the base of her spine went on from day to day. When Camilla bent over her bed calling out, 'Giuliana!' her sister tried to open her eyes and turn towards the voice. But she was overwhelmed by her weakness; her senses were possessed once more by a troubled stupor.

She was hungry, really hungry. A bestial craving for food tortured her empty stomach, gave to her mouth that vague movement of the jaws demanding something to chew, gave at times to the poor bones of her hands those prehensile contractions seen in the fingers of greedy monkeys at the sight of an apple. It was that rabid hunger of the convalescent recovering from typhus, that terrible greed for vital nourishment in all the cells of the body impoverished by a long illness. One meagre drop of blood remained, hardly circulating through her tissues; all activity in her poorly irrigated brain stagnated once more, as in a machine which lacks the motive force of liquid. Only, in that substance certain vibrations were now being confusedly produced, determining certain actions which had been habitual in her previous life; and the convalescent was not conscious at all of these mechanical workings. She spent most of her time reciting litanies; dividing into syllables words that made no sense; threatening to punish pupils; singing the five-syllabled lines of the stanzas of a hymn to Jesus. She kept making a pointing motion with the forefinger of her left hand, running it along the edge of the sheet, as if she meant with that sign to guide her pupils' eyes along the lines of print in a book. Then, sometimes, her voice was raised and took on an almost menacing solemnity, pronouncing the warning of the seven trumpets, remembering confusedly the words of Fra Bartolomeo da Saluzzo to sinners. Perhaps in her astonished eyes there was a vision of those old woodcuts full of misshapen angels trumpeting and demons put to flight. But she never had any sight in her eyes. Her heavy eyelids half covered the irises, those colourless irises, looking as if they were veiled in a yellowish mucus. She was stretched out in her bed, with her head resting on two pillows. During her illness she had lost almost all her hair; an ashen pallor – one of those pallors beneath which it looks as though no life could remain – was over her face, the hollows of her face; and her skull showed through it; and her skeleton showed through all the dryness of the skin which remained; and throughout that heap of bones the tissues still adhering to the places where it pressed upon the bed were degenerating. All that animated that ruin was an immense hunger, which tormented the intestines where the typhoidal ulcers were healing slowly.

Out of doors there was the Christmas novena, a beautiful celebration for old and young. There were certain clear, cold evenings when the whole region of Pescara was peopled with sailors and filled with the sound of bagpipes. The sharp scent of fish soup spread through the air from the open hovels. Slowly, at the windows, at the doors, in the streets, lights came on. The rosy sun lingered on the stone balconies of the Farina house, on the chimneys of the Memma house, on the bell tower of San Giacomo. Those illustrious heights shone like light-houses over the land in shadow. Then, all at once, night started to fill the firmament with stars; above the houses in Sant'Agostino a half-moon appeared from behind the ramparts between the red lamp and the telegraph-pole; it was crescent.

All that lively bustle rose up to Giuliana's room in a confused rumble like the sound of a beehive awakening.

The pastoral music of the bagpipes came nearer, from house to house, from door to door. There was a familiar and religious joy in those sounds which the peasants of Atina drew from a sheepskin and a set of hollow reeds. The convalescent heard, sat up in bed; that excite-ment raised in her once more the ghosts of other past excitements, and her eyes were filled with a holy vision of gleaming cribs and white processions of angels in pure blue skies. She began to sing lauds, holding out her arms, at times keeping her mouth open while her speech organs failed to produce a voice; she started to praise Jesus, uplifted by a sweet and ardent love, transported by the sound of the bagpipes coming nearer, dazzled by the holy pictures on the walls. She ascended into heaven, amid the music of the cherubim, in clouds of myrrh and incense.

'Hosanna!'

She had no voice. She held out her arms. Camilla, who was nearby, wanted to settle her down again on the pillows; she felt herself over-come by that blind enthusiasm of faith; her hands, her lips trembled. Giuliana fell back, spread out, with her head lolling, her throat and breast uncovered, with only the whites of her eyes showing against the general pallor, smiling at something invisible, in the attitude of a virgin martyr. The bagpipes went past; later in the night the sailors went past, bawling drinking-songs as they returned to their boats at Pescara.

3

The instinct for food reawakened and became intense, as she became more conscious of things. When the warm scent of bread arose from Flajano's oven, Giuliana asked for some; she asked in the tones of a starving beggar, stretching out her hand in supplication to her sister. She devoured the food rapidly, enjoying it in a savage way and with the whole of her being, looking about her suspiciously to see if anyone was trying to snatch the food out of her hands.

Her convalescence was long and slow; but already a gentle feeling of relief was starting to spread through her limbs, to clear her head. Through the wholesome nutrition of albumen and muscular flesh, a fresh supply of blood was produced. Her lungs, now greatly expanded with air, enlivened her blood which was itself charged with nourishment; and the tissues irrigated by the warm and rapid flow re-established themselves and took on some colour, their bedsores were healed and gradually new flesh formed over where they had been; with that new influx of life her brain was functioning properly; and the innervation of the sense organs, which were no longer troubled, made all sensation clear; and on her skull the roots of her hair were sprouting thickly; from that reordering of the mechanical laws of life, from that unfolding, provoked by the illness, of previously latent energies, from that intense desire which the convalescent had of living and feeling herself alive, from all those things, slowly, as if by a second birth, a better creature arose.

It was the beginning of February.

From her bed Giuliana could see the top of the Portanova Arch, the reddish bricks among which grass was growing, the crumbling capitals where the swallows had hung their nests. The Sant'Anna violets in the cracks in the fastigium were not yet in bloom. The sky above spread out in a serene beatitude of colour; and through the air from time to time came the blare of the bands in the arsenal.

It was then that, with something of a feeling of wonder, she went over her previous existence. It almost seemed as if that past did not belong to her, was not hers; she was now separated from those memories by an immeasurable distance, a dreamlike distance. She was no longer certain in her reckoning of time; she had to look at the things around her, make a strong mental effort, take a long time to get herself together, in order to remember. She put her fingers to her temples where thin hair was beginning to grow, and a vague, absent-minded smile brushed across her lips, showed fleetingly in her eyes.

'Ah!' she murmured hoarsely, and started moving her fingers to her temples again, gently.

It had been a sad and unvarying existence, in those three rooms, among all the little misshapen statues of saints, among all the pictures of Our Lady, among all those infants spelling out in chorus for five hours every day the same words written in chalk on the blackboard. Like the legendary glorious martyrs, like St Thecla of Iconium and St Euphemia of Chalcedon, the two sisters had consecrated their virginity to the Heavenly Bridegroom, to the bridal bed of Jesus.[10] They had mortified their flesh by dint of privations and prayers, breathing ecclesiastical air, incense, and the smell of burning candles, feeding themselves on vegetables.

They had benumbed their spirits by that long, arid exercise of spelling out words syllable by syllable, by that cold distillation of words, by that mechanical labour of needle and thread on the eternal white linen cloths smelling of lavender and sanctity. But their hands went to touch their pupils' foreheads, in a sudden burst of tenderness. They taught a small amount of doctrine, the little songs of religion; they made all those joyful heads bow beneath Lenten admonitions; they spoke of sin, of the horrors of sin, of eternal sufferings, in stern voices, while all those big eyes filled with wonder, and all those rosy lips fell open in amazement. Through the lively fantasies of the children the things around them took on life; from the depths of the old pictures issued certain yellowish profiles of mysterious saints; and the Nazarene, crowned with thorns and drops of blood, was looking at them from all sides with His dying eyes, persecuting them; and in the huge fireplace every puff of smoke took on an atrocious shape. So they filled those ignorant souls with faith.

Now the memory of that sterile life came back to trouble Giuliana. She went back, she went back to her most distant years through a natural tendency of the spirit, she fled to the source; and a sudden fullness of exultation flooded through her, as if in one instant all her infancy flowed back into her heart.

'Camilla! Camilla!' she called out. 'Where are you?'

Her sister did not reply, she was not in the other room; she had perhaps gone out, to church, to vespers. Then the convalescent felt tempted to put her feet to the ground, to try to walk on the floor, just as she was, alone.

She smiled the timid smile of a child starting upon a difficult undertaking; she half closed her eyes in the new delight which that thought gave her; her fingers felt her knees, her thin ankles, in concentration, as if estimating her strength; and she laughed, laughed because laughing imbued her with a pleasant languor, a subtle pleasure, quivering throughout her being.

A shaft of sunlight grazed the window-sill and struck the water in a basin in one corner; the moving reflection reached the wall, like a fine thread of gold. A flock of doves flew across and settled on the arch; it seemed an augury. Gently she pushed aside the covers, and hesitated for a moment; sitting on the edge of the bed, with the toes of her scraggy yellow foot she felt for the woollen slipper. She found one, she found the other; but now she was overcome by a tenderness that filled her eyes with tears, and everything shook in front of her in an indistinct light, as if things around were becoming airy and evanescent. Her cheeks were streaked with warm, salt tears, which came to rest at her mouth; she drank some of them, and tasted them. Outside, the doves fluttered off the arch and into the air again. Giuliana, with a movement of her jaws, swallowed the lump in her throat; then she rested on the edge of the bed, pushed on it, and finally got to her feet; and she smiled with tearful eyes, looking at herself. She did not know that she was so weak that she could not stand up on her legs; she had a strange sensation of tingling in her shins, of tickling in her muscles, like that sensation of a wound which comes when a broken bone has not yet quite knitted. She tried to take a step, she put out her foot, timidly: she was afraid, and sat down again on the edge of the bed, looking about her as if to be sure that no one was watching. Then she looked for something to aim for – the window – and began again, gently, with her eyes fixed on the foremost foot, balancing, pulling her green shawl around her breast, rather overcome by the cold. She was seized by fear all of a sudden, while she was still halfway: she swayed, waved her hands about, turned back towards the bed, took three or four rapid steps, fell back on the edge of the bed. She remained there a moment, catching her breath; she went back under the covers where there was still some warmth, wrapped herself up, and collected her thoughts, shivering.

'How weak I am, Lord!...'

She gazed in curiosity at the floor, that place where she had taken those steps, as if she were trying to find her footprints there.

4

She said nothing to her sister about this first attempt. When she heard Camilla coming back in, she closed her eyes, remained motionless as though asleep, taking a strange pleasure in that deception, suppressing with an effort the laugh that tickled her upper chest and rose to her lips. She took pleasure in that little secret: every day she waited with a restless desire for the time when Camilla would go down the stairs; she remained for a moment listening, sitting on the bed, until she could hear her sister descending slowly; then she would get up, stifling her bursts of laughter, leaning against the walls and the furniture, emitting low cries of fear whenever her knees threatened to buckle, whenever she lost her balance.

Almost always at that time of day the smell of bread rose from Flajano's oven to stir her. She went to the window to get some air; she experienced torment mixed with sensual pleasure as she breathed in that wholesome emanation, with her mouth watering and her eyes shining with desire. At that time she was seized with a rage to rummage through everything, to put her hands everywhere, dragging herself about less slowly, making futile and angry attempts on the locks whose keys Camilla had taken with her. On one occasion, in the back of a drawer in a little table, she found an apple and sank her teeth into it greedily. For some time, under the harsh regime of her convalescence, she had not tasted any fruit. That fruit had the perfume of fresh roses, that concentrated perfume which wrinkled and discoloured apples sometimes have. She searched round the drawer again, in hope; but all she found was a kind of greenish pod, unopened, which probably should have contained a set of seeds; and she took it, gazed at it curiously, hid it under her pillow.

That was how she spent that time, in secret, with the bitter enjoyment which little boys who are on the road to recovery get from forbidden things, infractions of the doctor's orders, small thefts. Her only witness was a cat, speckled all over like a snake, which sometimes walked round Giuliana mewing in a friendly way or stopping and stiffening in a vain attempt to snatch one of the doves outside when they flew onto the arch. Little by little Giuliana grew to love that discreet companion. She took him into the warmth of her bed, she whispered unconnected words to him, she gazed at him for long periods while he licked his paws with his rosy tongue, proffered his lizard-like throat to her blandishments, a yellowish throat which throbbed with a sound that was·both hoarse and sweet, like the cooing of turtle doves in the woods. Perhaps through a natural recurrence of her former mysticism, she loved the translucent flashes of the animal's eyes in the half-light, those splashes of phosphorus which emanated from a mysterious and silent shape in the half-light.

Camilla regarded all these strange predilections of her sister's with a sort of mistrust and silent regret, but she held her tongue. And slowly, almost insensibly, those two souls separated, distanced themselves from each other simply by what they denied each other.

Previously they had lived continually in a communion of habits and feelings, because in them every difference of disposition and every rebellion was balanced and ironed out in the one faith, in the indestructible veneration of Christ's deity, in that contemplation which had become the aim of their life. But as they were completely absorbed in this veneration, the ties of consanguinity between them had gradually been, one might almost say, covered up and overcome by those of their common religion; and so there was never any effusion of tenderness, never any outburst of intimacy or of memory or hope, as between sisters. They were co-religionists, members of the great family of Jesus spread out across the earth and yearning for heaven.

And so gradually, through the renewal brought about first by her illness and then by the course of treatment, Giuliana revealed unexpected attitudes of mind and unaccustomed habits, the estrangement became inevitable, and the voice of their blood relationship, having been lulled to sleep, could not be raised against it.

5

The pupils returned. They arrived one morning at the beginning of March. Giuliana had risen from her bed; she was sitting on the edge of it, with the warmth of the sun on the back of her neck and her shoulders. There was in the room the sour smell of the vinegar which Camilla had poured into the musty inkwells; and very occasionally through the windows the wind brought the perfume of the violets already blooming on the arch.

Then the children burst into the room. At first there were little heads jostling in the doorway, trying to see above each other, then there was hesitation, timidity, a sort of ingenuous wonder at the sight of the pallid and gaunt teacher whom the pupils hardly recognised.

But Giuliana smiled, moved by a sudden perturbation in her blood; Giuliana called them over, mixed up the names which sprang to her lips, and held out her hands to them. One, two, three at a time the children went up to her, they wanted to take her hands to press their lips upon them, they repeated the good wishes they had been taught at home, swallowing the syllables in their haste.

'No, no, no more!' exclaimed Giuliana, overcome, but surrendering her hands to those warm, soft mouths. She almost felt she was dying.

'Camilla, stop them, stop them.'

Every child brought a gift; there were flowers, there was fruit. The violets' perfume had suddenly spread through the air, and in that perfume, in that light, all those children's faces, reddened with good plebeian blood, were smiling.

Then, in the other room, school began. The first class were saying aloud the vowels and diphthongs, and the second class the syllables;

and over that clear chorus from time to time Camilla's admonitions could be heard.

'*La, le, li, lo, lu…*'

In the intervals of silence came the sound of Matteo Puriello hammering on his soles or Jece's loom knocking.

'*Va, ve, vi, vo, vu…*'

Then Giuliana felt annoyed. The monotonous noises and voices made her head feel unpleasantly heavy, and made her sleepy, while she wanted to be awake, feeling around her the breathing of the children, the joyful breath of those lives.

'*Bal, bel, bil, bol, bul…*'

She took the flowers and put them in a glass full of water to keep them fresh. Then she smelt them for a long time. She remained with her nostrils among all that freshness, with her eyes closed, concentrating on the sinful scent.

'*Gra, gre, gri, gro, gru…*'

A great white cloud covered the sun. Giuliana went to the window, she looked out of it to gaze down into the square. In front of her, Donna Fermina Memma in a pink dress stood on the balcony among the vases of carnations; and a group of officers went by beneath her, laughing and making a rattling noise with their sabres on the pavement. Further away, in the public gardens, the lilies were flowering, the crest of the gigantic pine was shaking in the wind. Out from Lucitino's bar came Verdura, the eternal drunkard, staggering and shouting.

Giuliana drew back; it was the first time, after so long, that she had looked down at the square. She seemed to be very, very high, looking down; she felt a touch of vertigo.

'*Nar, ner, nir, nor, nur…*'

Inside, the chorus went on and on and on.

'*Pla, ple, pli, plo, plu…*'

Giuliana felt herself suffocating, fainting under that torture: her poor weakened nerves were giving way. The chorus continued, to the rhythm of Camilla's stick beating on the table, implacably.

'*Ram, rem, rim, rom, rum…*'

'*Sat, set, sit, sot, sut…*'

Then Giuliana was shaken by a sudden fit of sobbing which made her fall onto the bed. She went on sobbing just as she fell, face down, her arms flung open, pressing her face against the pillows, without being able to stop herself.

'*Tal, tel, til, tol, tul…*'

6

All her hair had grown back, curly and dark as before. She was now very curious to see herself in a mirror, because Rosa Catena, with one of those affectations which always revealed what a loose woman she had been, had passed her hands over her body, saying, 'Beautiful!'

And so she waited until Camilla had gone out; then she got out of bed, and took down from the wall one of those rococo mirrors framed in gold and tarnished with green spots; she dusted it with a corner of the bedcover and looked into it, smiling. Her whole neck was bare, and on her neck some bluish veins stood out, there was something goat-like in her long narrow head, her mouth was delicate, her chin sharp, and her eyes dark like her hair, but tending more to yellow. Her transparent pallor and her smile lent a new grace, a new youthfulness to her twenty-seven years.

She went on looking at herself for a long time; and she enjoyed moving the mirror slowly away and seeing the image disappear in that rather glaucous light as though behind a veil of sea water, and then re-emerge. Vanity overcame her and preoccupied her. She became aware of so many little things with which she had previously never bothered; for example, a mole like a lentil which blemished the skin on her left temple, and a light scar which ran across the arch of one eyebrow. She remained like that for a long time. Then, struck with unexpected joy, she looked around for some other pleasure.

That vegetable cupule which she had found in the back of a drawer had opened into two valves, revealing a cluster of blackish seeds. Every seed seemed to be connected to very fine filaments of a silvery brightness; and the cluster remained close-packed. But as soon as Giuliana puffed at it, a cloud of white down rose into the air and scattered here and there, glittering: they were like dandelion seeds. The seeds seemed to have wings, they looked like slender, evanescent insects which dissolved in the sun's rays or looked like scarcely visible swansdown; they billowed, they floated downwards again, they got tangled in Giuliana's hair, they brushed her face, they covered her all over. She laughed as she defended herself against that invasion, trying to drive off that down that tickled her skin and stuck to her hands; but her laughter prevented her puffing.

In the end she stretched herself out on the bed, and let all that soft snowfall descend upon her slowly. She kept her eyes half closed to prolong the pleasure; and gradually she was overcome by drowsiness, she felt herself submerged in a deep feather bed. The light coming into the room was that of pale, bright afternoons in March, when the cheerful, rosy light of the sun laughs modestly and fades away like a forerunner of the dawn which covers the whole sky.

Camilla found her sister still asleep with the mirror at her side, with the seeds in her hair.

'Oh, Lord Jesus! Oh, Lord Jesus!' she murmured between her teeth, putting her hands together in an act of bitter compassion.

That Christian woman had just come from church, where she had sung the litanies for the Annunciation and had heard the sermon on the message of the Archangel to the handmaid of the Lord. *Ecce ancilla Domini.*[11] The preaching brother's eloquence had intoxicated her; certain admonitory words were still ringing in her ears.

Giuliana awakened at that moment with a long, voluptuous yawn, and stretched her limbs.

'Ah! Is it you, Camilla?' she said, rather confused at her presence.

'It's me, it's me! You will be lost, poor thing, you will be lost!' exclaimed the pious woman, pointing to the mirror on the bed. 'You have in your hands the devil's instrument…'

And, excited by her first outburst, she went on, she raised her voice, she threw in ardent sentences from the sermon; with great airy gestures she urged the threats of eternal punishment, addressing herself not only to Giuliana, but going so far as to admonish the whole universe of sinners.

'*Memento! Memento!*'[12]

Giuliana could not hear anything now, because all that outcry had deafened her.

Suddenly from one corner of the square the military band burst out in a blare of twenty trumpets.

7

The highest room of the house was low and narrow, with its ceiling beams blackened by smoke, full of the stench of onions, washing-up, and burnt coal. The copper vases hung in order on the wall, without a sparkle; the Castelli plates were arranged in order on the shelf with their cheerful pictures of flowers, birds, and men's heads; the ancient brass lamps, the empty bottles, vegetable leaves, no longer fresh, were strewn over the tables; and dominating everything was St Vincent, their protector, represented with a large book in his hand and the red flame in the middle of his head.

There, in the old days, Giuliana, in among the clouds of steam and the fumes of vegetables, had often been struck by the choruses of bawdy songs and the widespread cackles of laughter following them, which came through the little high window. The songs and the laughter grew louder on summer evenings, to the accompaniment of guitars, and the thumping of feet dancing on the ground. All the sounds of life in the most wretched of slums rose, at certain times of the day, to that height and made the poor brides of Christ tremble with horror as they humbly bent over the clay pans full of the pulses and vegetables which went with their hermit-like innocence. But now, in this fresh time of gaiety, when one day Giuliana heard those voices, she felt a strong impulse to look out.

Camilla was not at home; it was the fifth Sunday of Lent. A pleasanter warm breath in the air, after the showers, showed how soon it would be April; and in that air the maiden sensed more fully and clearly her rebirth. And, at leisure, taking a turn through the rooms, it was natural that her curiosity should make her look out, seized by the unwholesome fascination which lewd spectacles exercise even on modest minds.

By climbing onto a chair she reached up to the opening; but before she looked out she was struck by a fit of shaking, and as she stood on the chair she turned round, afraid that someone might catch her in the act.

Everything around was quiet: every now and then a tiny drop of water could be heard falling from a basin on high. From outside the voices rose and enticed her.

Giuliana was reassured, and she looked out. In the alley, the rotted rubbish had fermented in the rain like yeast; over the pavement was a black mire, in which leftovers of fruit, remains of herbs, rags, worn-out shoes, brims of hats, all the rotten trash which poverty throws into the street were mixed together. On that cesspool, where the sun was breeding insects and foul vapours, a string of tiny suffocated houses backed onto the barracks. From all the windows, however, from all the cracks, carnations, spilling over the edges of their vases, were overflowing; and the big pink and red flowers hung down in the sun, blooming splendidly. And among those flowers appeared the flabby painted faces of the prostitutes, lewd songs floated past them, and bursts of guttural laughter; and down on the pavement, under the iron bars of the barracks, other women were offering themselves to the soldiers, talking in loud voices, provocatively.

And the soldiers, sensing in their blood all the ills of Venus flourishing once more in the spring, stretched out their hands between the bars just to grope something, their blazing eyes devouring those women already worn out years ago by the lust of such a drunken rabble and so many sodden louts.

Giuliana stood there stupefied at the spectacle of all that obscene corruption fermenting in the good Lenten sunlight and rising up to her. She did not draw back from it yet; but as she raised her eyes she saw in a dormer window of the barracks a fair-haired man looking at her and smiling. She hurriedly got down from the chair, paler than before, thinking that she could hear Camilla's voice. She ran into her own room, and threw herself onto the bed, bewildered, breathless, as if someone had been pestering her with threats.

8

After that day, all the time, every moment when Camilla was not at home, a violent desire drew her towards that sight. She fought against it at first, vainly, without strength, allowing herself to be overcome. She went there with the mistrustful anxiety of someone going to a lovers' meeting; she stayed there a long time, behind the crumbling venetian blind, while the brothel-like miasma disturbed her and corrupted her.

She spied on everything, keeping her eyes sharp, trying to penetrate indoors, trying to discover something through the carnations that obscured the windows. The sun was hot and heavy; swarms of insects whirled about in the air. At intervals, when a man came into the alley, there came from the windows the cries of those waiting; half-naked women, with their breasts uncovered, went out to offer themselves. The man disappeared through one of the doors with the woman he had chosen. Those who were disappointed hurled scorn and laughter after the couple, and went to lie in ambush again among the carnations.

And that was how lust was kindled in Giuliana. The need for love, latent before, now rose up throughout her being, and became a torment, an incessant, ferocious torture against which she could not defend herself.

She was filled with a warm gush of health; a sudden *joie de vivre* set her blood coursing, filled her breast with a feeling like the flutter of wings, put a song into her mouth. At times one breath, one of those tiny fluctuations of air which spread out beneath the sun, the song of a beggar, a smell, a mere nothing sufficed to make her fall into a vague swoon, an abandonment in which she seemed to feel on all her limbs the caressing movement of the velvet skin of a mature fruit. She was lost and gliding into unknown depths of sweetness. The irritation brought on by self-restraint, the unwonted superabundance of juices, that continual tensing of her nerves under stimulation held her in a sort of daze rather like the first stages of drunkenness; she felt as though vapours were rising from her heart to her brain and turning her vision red. The past disappeared, drowsed in the depths of her memory, and never revived. And all the time, everywhere, desire set snares for her;

the saints on the walls, the Madonnas, the naked crucified Christs, the little misshapen wax figures, all those things around, took on for her an appearance of impurity. Impurity emanated from all those things and breathed on her ardently. And then there was a final battle, in which her conscience bowed, her will yielded, her senses triumphed.

'Well, now I'm going into the street,' she said to herself, resisting no longer.

Then her hands trembled on the door as she opened it; shooting the bolt presented her with another obscene image. She turned back, threw herself almost fainting onto the bed, livid, beneath the fantasy of a man.

9

On Palm Sunday she went out for the first time in so many months, because Camilla wished to take her to give thanks to the Lord for her recovery. Giuliana appeared once the bells started to ring. The whole countryside was smiling under the great Easter smile of the April sun. All the people about were crowding the roads, carrying olive branches as a sign of peace.

Now she had to dress in her best clothes: the people on the roads would look at her as she passed. She was suddenly seized by a frenzy of vanity; she locked herself in her room; she searched in the depths of the chest for the brightest clothes. A strong odour of camphor arose from those old fabrics preserved there for years; there were wide skirts in flowered silk, green and violet and iridescent, which in the old days had perhaps been puffed out around the hips of new brides by crinolines; there were long bodices with puff sleeves, dove-grey capes edged with white lace, veils interwoven with silver threads, fine cloth collars embroidered in hemstitching; all dead things, worn out by use, awkward, stained with damp.

Giuliana tried to make her choice, as though guided by a new instinct, covering her hands with the scent of camphor as she searched. All that useless silk and those veils irritated her; in the end she found nothing that suited her. She closed the chest angrily, pushed it back under the bed with her foot. The bells were ringing for the first time.

She hastily put on her usual ash-grey dress, in front of Camilla, biting her lips to keep back her tears.

The bells were calling. Along the roads the bundles of palms shone with a moving silver glitter; above every group of peasants arose a forest of little branches; and a pure mild Christian blessing spread through all the air from those forests, as if the Galilean were approaching, the poor gentle king seated on an ass among his crowd of disciples, coming to meet the hosannas of the redeemed people. *Benedictus qui venit in nomine Domini. Hosanna in excelsis!*[13]

In the church there was an immense crowd of people, an immense forest of palms. By one of those irresistible currents which are created in crowds of people, Giuliana was separated from Camilla; she stayed alone in that swarm, in the middle of all that touching, in the middle of all that shoving, of all those breaths. She tried to open a way for herself; her hands encountered men's backs, and other warm hands whose touch disturbed her. She felt her face brushed by an olive leaf, her step impeded by a knee, an elbow pushing into her side, her breast outraged, her shoulders outraged by unfamiliar pressures. Beneath the smell of incense, beneath the blessed palms, in the mystical half-light, in all that pack of Christian men and women, the friction caused little erotic sparkles which multiplied; secret lovers found each other and came together again. Country girls passed by Giuliana with palms on their breasts, with a fleeting smile in the whites of their eyes for the lovers who were behind them, seducing them; and she felt love passing by all around her, she found herself putting her body between those bodies searching for each other, she was an obstacle to those gestures of people trying to touch each other, she prevented those hands clasping, those arms linking. But something of those interrupted caresses went into her blood. At one point she came face to face with a fair-haired soldier; she almost rested her head on his tunic, because a column of people was pushing her from behind. She raised her eyes; and the young man smiled just as he had smiled that day from the dormer window of the barracks. Behind, the shoving continued; the fumes of incense spread more thickly, and in the background the deacon sang:

'*Procedamus in pace.*'[14]

And the chorus responded:

'*In nomine Christi. Amen.*'[15]

That was the announcement that the procession was beginning, and it put the people into an enormous commotion. Instinctively, violently, without thinking, Giuliana attached herself to the man, as if she already belonged to him; she let herself almost be lifted up by those arms which held her sides, she felt in her hair the virile breath smelling faintly of tobacco. And that was how she walked – weakened, exhausted, oppressed by that voluptuousness which had come upon her unexpectedly, seeing nothing but a dazzling light in front of her.

Then the thurifer came from the high altar scattering clouds of sweet sky-blue smoke upon the people; and a procession, all in white, uncoiled in the centre of the church. The celebrants had olive branches in their hands and they were singing.

10

All of Holy Week watched over Giuliana's love with its complicit shadows. The churches were immersed in the twilight of the Passion; the crucifixes on the altar were covered in violet cloths; the tombs of the Nazarene were surrounded by great white grasses grown in cellars; the air was loaded with the scent of flowers and benzoin.

Giuliana waited there, on her knees, until a light footstep behind her made her start. She could not turn round, because Camilla was watching her; but she felt herself quite embraced by that man's glance, as if by a gentle fire, and a tender desire swept through her flesh. Then she fixed the burning candles in tiers on a wooden triangle near the altar. The priests were singing in front of a large book; and one by one the candles burned out. Only five of them remained, only two of them remained; from the depths of the chapels darkness advanced upon the people in prayer. Eventually the last tiny flame died out; all the benches resounded with the beating of twigs. In the darkness, Giuliana, the moment she felt herself touched by two searching hands, leapt up from the floor with a bewildered start. Then, as she was going out of the church, the thought of having violated a sacred place filled her with remorse: suddenly, from a level below consciousness, the idea of punishment sprang up again. Then it was all like a dream in which the livid figure of the dead Jesus and the rattle of the beatings and the shudder of the aroused flesh and the heavy scent of the flowers and the breath of that fair-haired man were mingled in a dubious feeling of pain and pleasure.

11

But when Jesus rose in triumph into the glory of heaven, the paschal aromas were no longer a comfort to Giuliana's love. Then the theatre of love was the dominion of stray cats and earthbound doves. Sweet signals came to Giuliana's window from the dormer window; in between, the brothel was sunk like a ditch of slimy water on whose banks flowers grew, nourished by its putrefaction. The doves flew over it in a glitter of green and grey plumage.

The lover bore a fine ancient name, Marcello, and he had beautiful red and silver edging on the sleeves of his tunic. He wrote letters full of eternal fire, containing vehement sentences which gave to the loved one swoons of tenderness and voluptuous tremors which she could hardly contain. Giuliana read those pages in secret, she kept them in her bosom night and day; owing to the warmth, the violet writing was imprinted on her skin, and it was like a noble tattoo of love, in which she rejoiced. Her replies went on for ever: all the grammatical knowledge of a teacher, the whole treasure of psalmodic apostrophes of a pious woman, all the fluent sentimentality of a retarded maiden was poured out onto the pages of school exercise books lined in deep blue. While she was writing, she was taken out of herself, she felt herself carried along on a wave of sonorous verbosity: it almost seemed as if a new faculty were being exercised in her, and taking a maniacal form, all of a sudden. That large deposit of mystical lyricism accumulated by the reading of prayer-books during so many years of fidelity to the Heavenly Bridegroom, now, roused by the tumult of earthly love, rose up in confusion and, going through new levels of consciousness and combining itself with strange elements, was taking on, one might almost say, a flavour of fresh profanity. In this way the tearful invocations of

Jesus changed into sighs of hope for the joys of embraces that were not ethereal, the offering up of the flower of the soul to the Supreme Good changed into tender dedications of the flesh to the fair-haired lover's desire, and the aphrodisiacal light of the moon was encircled with all the epithets which make the Holy Spirit radiant; and spring zephyrs were not lacking to snatch a fragrance from the banquets in Paradise.

12

The go-between was one of those men who look as though they have grown up, like mushrooms, out of the dampness of the dirty street, and whose whole appearance seems to be tinged with their native mud; one of those grey men who insinuate themselves everywhere, who are always to be found where there is a cent to be gained, a little grease to lick up, a rag to pilfer – today rag-and-bone men and tomorrow procurers of maidservants or whores, today false brokers of merchandise and tomorrow catchers of stray dogs.

This fellow had an operatic name – Lindoro: from the Hospital district to the rampart of Sant'Agostino this name had acquired great popularity. This fellow was born from the coupling of a strolling clarinet-player with a common fruit-seller, and he had inherited his father's nomadic instincts and his mother's innate greed for money. To begin with he had dragged himself through the filth of all the houses, with his brush and basket; he had then been a kitchen-boy in a tavern, where soldiers and sailors threw the last drops from their glasses and the bones from badly fried fish into his face. He had sunk from the tavern to a baker's, where he pushed the loaves into the flames with a long shovel, all night, sweating, going blind. From the baker's he had passed into the office of the public lamplighter, damaging one of his shoulders under the weight of the portable ladder. Expelled from that office for extracting petrol from the great white zinc containers, he started to chance his arm on the streets, buying and selling old clothes, performing the most menial tasks in all the poorer homes, offering his services to soldiers and sailors as a pimp, struggling to earn a crust.

Every job had left its imprint on his body and his soul – a habitual gesture, the development of a particular muscle, the weakness of an organ, a certain hardening, a cadence in the voice, a cant phrase. He was short and thin, with an enormous head that was almost bald, with patches of thin hair on his cheeks, and pimples among the bristles. His clothing was hybrid and changeable; he had put on all the fashions, one on top of another in contrast: long yellowish aristocratic overcoats and trousers covered with patches, shameful felt hats and abject slippers, bright metal buttons, panels of white bone, army stripes, lace – that jumble of worn-out wealth and despicable poverty which clutters up the back of a Jewish rag-and-bone man's shop.

13

This fellow was now the pander. He carried Marcello's letters, together with the containers of water from Pescara, up to Giuliana's home, and went down with the containers empty and letters in reply. When she heard him coming up the stairs, Giuliana turned pale; she found pretexts to get rid of Camilla, to be alone with that man who brought water and joy. Their moments of contact were rapid and on the sly; there passed between her and the pander those sidelong glances of understanding, those fleeting hints given by facial muscles, those low monosyllables, so helpful to human wiles, and which in the long run create ties between the deceivers, where they are of different sexes, determining certain remarkable correspondences in their bodily movements, which can sometimes be the cause of sensual awakening. For this reason, something of Lindoro's influence gradually penetrated into Giuliana's love; a sort of familiarity was established little by little between the lover and the ambassador. If this fellow arrived while Camilla was absent, she pressed questions upon him; when she spoke she came so close to him that he could feel her breath, and sometimes she unconsciously put a hand on his shoulder. Lindoro gave full rein to his vulgar loquacity, interposing cant expressions, indecent reticences, shrewd revealing smiles, ambiguous gestures, little smackings of the tongue and lips.

He pimped artistically, he knew how to insinuate corruption into

Giuliana's mind, he knew how to draw the prey slowly into Marcello's trap. And Giuliana listened intently, with a growing flame in the depths of her eyes, and in her mouth the dryness produced by lascivious excitement, without interrupting him any more. Lindoro was immediately aware that he had aroused the woman's lust; and, in the presence of that figure leaning forward in her perturbation, his masculinity was aroused all of a sudden, and he was strongly tempted to pluck that flower which he was preparing for another's pleasure; but the fear rising from the depths of his cowardice held him back and froze his ardour.

And so eventually Giuliana had agreed to a meeting with Marcello. It was to take place in an out-of-the-way house in the district, down a deserted alley, where no one would catch sight of them; it was arranged for a Sunday in June, when Camilla would be spending a long time in church, and Lindoro would keep good watch.

In the days before that great event Giuliana was subject to a bitter excitement, to a kind of fever that at times made her teeth chatter, her face flush, and the roots of the hairs on her neck bristle. She could not now keep still, she could not remain seated, a rage for movement ran through all her limbs. In the schoolroom, amid the regular chorusing of her pupils, amid that continual dripping of syllables, a sudden mad rage of rebellion would dazzle her sight, and she would have liked to jump in among the children, ruffle all their hair with her hands, overturn the blackboard, the tables, the benches, utter shouts, break something into bits, forget herself. Beneath Camilla's cold, searching glance she almost fainted through agony, anger, and the previous immense effort of dissimulation.

Then, when Camilla went out, she bustled about through all the rooms, moved chairs, gnawed flowers, drank at one gulp large glasses of water, looked at herself in the mirror, went to the window, threw herself across the bed, gave vent in a thousand ways to her restlessness, the exuberance of her sensual vitality. Her whole body, in the delayed ferment of her virginity, had been enriched and expanded; she was like one of those blood-red bursts of autumn blossom, when the plant explodes as it feels a last current of vegetable strength invest those roots which are so lethargic as to be almost dead in the ground. All the pores in her body exhaled, irradiated scarcely restrained voluptuousness; in all her gestures, in her whole attitude, in all her slightest motions, a spontaneous aphrodisiacal glamour, an involuntary impudence revealed itself independently of the presence of a man. She was quite saturated with desire; the yellowish fibrils of her irises dilated, and spurted out flashes; her lower lip, tormented with gnawing, jutted out, wet and vermilion; the glaucous networks of her veins stood out on her neck, and sometimes, at sudden movements, certain sets of nerves quivered. Her head was not beautiful, she did not have the regular features, the olive splendour of certain peoples of the Abruzzi, their pure lines of nose and chin developing elegantly into a Latin fullness of face. But, unconsciously, beneath the awkwardness of her grey dresses, beneath the feebleness of the ill-arranged folds, she concealed a statuesque magnificence in her torso and her legs.

It was the beginning of June; summer was arising out of spring, like an aloe from a field of grass. What with the sea and the river, all the land of Pescara was enjoying the salty breezes and the fluvial chill, as though it were stretching out its arms towards those natural boundaries of salt water and fresh water. All the blandishments of the weather were increased in Giuliana's room; shining insects dashed against the window-panes and rebounded like golden hail.

Giuliana, when she was alone, felt the need to stretch herself, to cast off her clothes, to lie down, and to feel all over her skin those unknown caresses that were fluttering in the air.

Slowly she began to undress, lazily and with soft gestures, her fingers taking a long time over the laces and clasps, making little listless efforts as she withdrew her arms from the sleeves, stopping in the middle and throwing back her head with its short curly hair, that head of a beautiful young man. Slowly, beneath the loving effort, from the shapelessness of the clothes, like a statue disinterred from the dross of time, her naked body was revealed. A heap of wool and coarse linen lay at the feet of the maiden who was thus purified, and from that heap, as from a pedestal, she arose into the light, holding her arms up like a crown, while at the contact with the air a scarcely visible vibration ran over her contours, grazing the skin. In that momentary attitude, all the lines of her back stretched and rose towards the encircled head; the gentle curve of her belly was smooth, not yet disfigured by conception; the curve of her ribs stood out. Then, if an insect came into the room, its buzzing gliding around and showing signs of touching her nakedness, that buzzing bewildered Giuliana; and now it became a matter of defending herself against the fearful stings; there were serpentine movements, muscles jerking under the skin, a frightened gathering together of her limbs, her ankles going because they were not strong enough for this game, leaps, quivers, all that sudden access of agility and that shivering of the skin which repugnance provokes in a woman.

Then, hot and excited by the movement, she felt fresh desires. She opened the door, cautiously and suspiciously, and she put her head out to look in the other room. There was a musty smell, that inanimate dreariness which schools have when there are no children there; on the square tablets the alphabet in block letters and the groups of diphthongs and syllables held silent dominion over the place. Giuliana advanced, her bare feet avoiding the spaces where tiles had been displaced, experiencing the hesitancy of someone walking for the first time barefoot on a rough surface and the confusion of a woman who no longer feels her clothes around her, impeding her as they usually do when she is walking. In this way she walked to the third room, where the water was, where the dampness gave her a sensation of coolness underfoot and where she felt her hair standing up at the thought that her lover might not be far from there. She soaked her hands in the water, splashed herself all over, bravely, catching her breath suddenly when a larger drop ran down her skin. She left that room, covered in dew: she was being tempted by the tall mirror on an old piece of furniture.

There was an old chest of drawers which still preserved some fragments of inlay here and there; the mirror, which was concealed by an overhanging cupboard, had a frieze round it of colours mixed with gold, and above it two decapitated little cherubs. Giuliana climbed up there, attracted by an irresistible feminine curiosity of seeing herself naked. Her body, still fresh and dripping, rose in the darkness of the mirror suffused by a pale silver shadow, softened by imperceptible touches of azure and green where the glass was particularly changed by time. She looked at herself, while the sexual instinct, as beauty unveiled

29

itself, made a lively and spontaneous smile spring to her lips. That smile, every movement of her muscles, seemed to make all the lines of her nudity tremble in the mirror like an image in water. Then she began a sort of conceited pantomime, looking at all her gestures reproduced in the sheet of glass, opening her lips to reveal her teeth, raising her arms to reveal her armpits, exhibiting her arched back and forcing her head to turn round. Eventually a mad burst of hilarity, in front of that spectacle she was making of herself, shook her whole body. Far in the background, behind the woman, was reflected from the opposite wall a tablet with the alphabet on it.

14

At that moment Lindoro, coming up with the containers, happened to knock at the door to the staircase. Giuliana shouted:

'Just a moment!'

She gathered up her clothes in a rush; she put them on in a rush; she went to open the door.

It was six in the evening; the white glare of the Brina Palace was coming into the room; the whole region of Pescara, very hospitable to swallows, was singing.

In the middle of the room the two of them, on their feet, were speaking about the imminent meeting. Lindoro was using his loquacity to try to overcome the maiden's final hesitancy, because he already had part of his pay, and he was enticed by the balance. His persuasive artifices enlivened his words, his eyes, his gestures. In his breath there was the smell of wine, and on his face little red and violet spots where he had recently shaved. While he spoke, he revealed a row of regular, sound teeth, one of those strong fences by which plebeian mouths are often fortified: this singularity showed up vividly against the general foulness of the man.

Giuliana interrupted him with her opposing doubts and fears; but already, now that a certain indecency, growing warmer gradually with the wine he had drunk, was working its way into the pimp's persuasions, she began to feel that influx of warmth around the eyes, that numbing of her tongue, those dull thuds in the blood, which are the symptoms of amorous excitement. She had retreated little by little to the wall, and was leaning against it. Through the openings which had been left here and there in her clothing from the rush to dress herself there were glimpses of her underclothes, the whiteness of that linen which seems to be part and parcel of feminine nudity. Her throat was uncovered, white and lined by the collar of Venus; only the toes of her stockingless feet were hidden in her slippers.

But involuntarily at one point, through that blind instinct a woman has for knowing when she is faced by a lustful man, her hand hastened to fasten the little hooks under her throat and on her breast. That action, with which Giuliana acknowledged the man behind the pimp, that sudden action made a surge of masculine pride gush forth from Lindoro's abject state. Ah, so he had been able to arouse a woman by himself? And he went closer; and, as the wine gave him courage, he was on that occasion not held back by any cowardly reserve.

And on that bewildered and powerless maiden he showed how brutal he could be.

15

Giuliana was left inert, under the first violent, divine effects of that natural act which had been performed, in a kind of rapture which could not be exhaled. She remained on the tiles for a long time, her clothes and her whole self disordered by that violation.

From time to time there was a quiver in the whites of her vacant eyes; tremors went along her arms, because her nerves were strained; nervous shudders furrowed her brow, causing her eyelids to flicker, the corners of her mouth to curve up, and her big toes to make vague tiny movements.

When she heard Camilla's footsteps on the stairs, she raised herself on one elbow from the depths of her languor; she quickly passed her hands over her rumpled dress; she found the words to tell her sister that a sudden fit of weakness had made her fall down in the middle of the room.

Outside it was getting dark: the deep glaucous coolness of the June evening, which came from the Adriatic, was spreading over the whole town. The square was full of voices and laughter; throughout the block could be heard the singing which welcomes Saturday's joyfulness. From the second-floor landing Teodora La Jece shouted.

'Camilla, Camilla, are you coming?'

Giuliana followed her sister, without speaking, without thinking. She found it difficult to remember; a sort of sluggishness still possessed her memory. Teodora La Jece filled her ears with a slanderous and impudent woman's chatter.

'Rachela Catena's daughter's getting married you know.'

'Ah.'

'Take Giovannino Speranza. You know, that redhead with the inn at Pesceria and the falling sickness, God help us!'

'Ah.'

'Another thing; Checchina Madrigale has cleared off again to Francavilla. You know her: that fat woman who lives at Gloria, dark, with a nose like a beak... that one.'

Teodora La Jece carried on. She had got into step with Giuliana. Camilla came a little behind, her head bent, without paying any attention to the sins of backbiting the weaver's tongue was committing against her neighbour. Everyone was taking the air in the streets; groups of women passed by, in linen dresses, with their arms bare to the elbows.

'Look at that frill on Graziella Potavigna. Look at Rosa Zazzetta, with one sergeant in front of her and one behind... Ah, don't you see?'

There followed then an account of crazy love affairs full of salacious indiscretions, almost whispered in her ear. By one of those acts of forgetfulness which are the refuge of some weak and uncertain natures, Giuliana immersed herself completely in the gossip, with a sort of feverish frenzy, not giving herself time to think back, questioning, urging Teodora on to chatter, dreading the intervals of silence, filling them with little bursts of laughter. She almost took a bitter enjoyment in listening to others being reviled.

'Oh! Here's Don Paolo!'

Along came Don Paolo in all his tranquillity, an octogenarian who was still as tart and flourishing as juniper, as joyful and wise as Pantagruel.

'Come with us, Don Paolo; we're taking a stroll.'

All the butchers, here and there along the road, had their fresh sides of beef hanging in the middle of their doorways: the bovine smell spread out from the disclosed innards and assailed the nostrils. Higher up, long strings of macaroni were lined up in the light of the moon which regarded them from the summit of a pole crowning the barracks. Groups of soldiers crowded round the fruit vendors, bawling.

'Let's go to the Bandiera,' said Teodora, letting Don Paolo and Camilla go in front.

Giuliana passed through all those noises and strong odours in a state of bewilderment. Eventually a vague sense of dismay began to rise from the depths, to twist her mouth when she laughed and when she spoke, and impede her tongue. Even certain little physical torments pestered her and brought her back to reality. She could no longer flee; words died on her lips, her throat was tickled with anguish, the spectre of something enormous and irremediable rose up before her. She felt now that she was dying from the effort of keeping on her feet, of putting one foot in front of the other: she felt she was being hissed at by all the animation in the street, that is by everyone.

'So, that boss-eyed husband, not knowing anything at all...' said Teodora, taking up once more the thread of the interrupted slander.

They walked through the Bandiera. To the left the pontoon-bridge spanned the river. On their other side, the dark, heavy structure of the bastion stood out in the dim light. The old iron cannons, planted with their muzzles in the ground, stretched out in a line and held the hawsers; huge iron anchors cluttered the wharf. On the decks of the boats drawn up on shore the sailors were eating and smoking beneath the sails; the blood-red of the illuminated sails was in contrast to the whiteness of the moon. Round the prows large spots of liquefied matter were slowly rising and falling.

'...sent for Don Nerèo Memma, just imagine!' continued the implacable Teodora.

'Who's talking about Dr Dulcamara?' asked Don Paolo, who had caught the name. He laughed with an open mouth: it was still well provided with ivory.

Giuliana felt nothing any more; she was as pale as the face of the moon. At first, all that great luminous peace raining down from the sky onto the river, and all those long traces of sea smells streaming through the coolness had almost given her an impression of joyful relief; because in the presence of that attractive scene the ghosts of desire in the depths of her mind recovered, and the height of feeling glittered again in the rays of the moon. Immediately she felt she was being suffocated, there was a confused tumult in which she was conscious of herself only because of the pounding of the arteries on her temples, because of that deafening murmur which seemed to spread and fill all the air at once. She could not feel firm ground beneath her feet; the edge of the water became hazy as she grew dizzy; the river came onto the road; water water water was spreading all around. Then, all at once, a sparkle of light came into her eyes, a trembling, growing will-o'-the-wisp which broke, interwove, faded, and melted and disappeared sinuously in the half-light. In that light the figure of Marcello appeared and disappeared, as rapidly and changeably as in a dream. The dizziness ceased. Giuliana recognised the reflection of the moon in the peaceful river; she went on walking, stunned, weakened, ready to faint almost.

'Tired are you then? You're not used to it, you know. Lean on me, lean on me,' said Teodora. 'Donna Mentina Ussoria's daughter, the smaller one, pock-marked, was just in front of the shop, you see, on the square…'

They had reached the *Finanzieri* barracks[16]. Great heaps of carobs gave out a powerful odour of tanned hides; and the street, strewn with oyster shells, was creaking under their feet. Two moorhens, by the bank, were fishing for eels, in silence, under the favourable light of the moon. But the sound of the sea filled the silence with grandeur: that they were near the mouth of the river was shown by the salt waves lapping over the gentle surface of the fresh water.

'Let's go back, young ladies,' said Don Paolo, taking a carob from the nearby pile.

Giuliana let herself be led. She found it hard to repress her difficulty in breathing, because now her state, in its urgent dreadfulness, was clear to her and was crushing all the longing and the tumultuous feelings which had been aroused in her in the voluptuousness of the moonlit night. She saw, in her obsessive thought, the figure of Lindoro rise and come alive; once more she felt herself seized and felt by those rough hands, suffocated by that breath hot with wine and lust, violated on the floor tiles of her room. But at that moment, she thought, she had not resisted, not called out, not made any attempt to oppose him; she had succumbed, powerless, not being able to make out anything any more, feeling nothing but a great joy mingled with pain flowing through her body, feeling nothing but the violence of repressed nature rebelling throughout her being. Then the reflection of that feeling disturbed her flesh anew with an infinite, languorous tenderness; and in her muddled consciousness she ceased to have any ideas of her own. It seemed to her that so many nocturnal things, like voices and wings, had come to beat against her temples, had come to tempt her, to make her shake and suggest words to her. She looked straight in front of her, pale, and with her eyes growing larger and darker. That is how she was: weak, uncertain, incapable of assessing freely any state of mind or any situation, swinging wretchedly between suggestions coming from the external world and her internal suffering.

'Hear how the wine makes people sing,' said Don Paolo, stopping.

In the boats the sailors were stretched out among the cordage, amid the smoke from Dalmatian tobacco, and they were singing about beautiful women, in a great chorus.

16

Camilla prayed for a long time at the prie-dieu, in a low voice, with her head bent and her hands joined; she lit the votive lamp to the Virgin Mary for it to burn through the night; then she gave way to sleep, holding the gentle heart of Jesus among the withered flowers on her breast. Her deep breathing was religious, as though it were brushing against the Sacred Host on its silver paten. On the vaulted ceiling the shadows followed the wavering of the tiny flame fed by oil; those dry sounds of swelling wood and gnawing woodworms, the mysterious creaking of old furniture in the night's calm, and the buzzing of mosquitoes broke the silence.

Giuliana was in the same bed, at Camilla's side, lying full length, without moving, without closing her eyes, because a deep sleepless weariness was in all her limbs and a continual vigilant anguish was torturing her wretched soul. She listened to the silence, she spied upon herself with anxious curiosity, as if to find out what changes had been made in her being.

Suddenly, in her sleep, Camilla started to murmur vague words, fragments of incomprehensible words, scarcely moving her lips, emitting long breaths in which could be heard half-extinguished sounds, and the hoarse gurgles of unformed words and the accents of broken words. Her head, gaunt, pinched, one might almost say sculptured and chiselled severely by penitence and fasting, yellow in the light of the lamp, lay on the pillow's whiteness like the poorly gilded effigy of a saint on the starburst of a nimbus. Little violet shadows marked the inside of her nostrils, the furrows of her stretched neck which was covered with sinews, the hollows in her cheeks, the eye sockets from which bulged the great balls of the eyes covered in the eyelids' soft skin. Thus she looked like the corpse of a martyr whose spirit had ascended to God.

Although it was not the first time she had heard such nocturnal soliloquies, Giuliana felt her scalp grow cold: a sudden terror attacked her and weighed her down. Instinctively she cowered, tried to distance herself from her sister's body, withdrawing to the very edge of the bed; she remained motionless, suspended in the intervals of silence, with her eyes fixed on the sleeper's mouth, feeling her heart miss a beat in her breast when those lips moved to proffer more words. She did not understand; but there was something distantly profound and solemn in that broken murmuring, as if a mysterious, supernatural phenomenon were rising from that inert, unconscious body which spoke without hearing its own voice. A breath like the breath from a sepulchre passed through the room; in Giuliana's disturbed imagination, flickering shadows took on the fearful and threatening shapes of spectres; the air seemed furrowed by unknown noises. All the things in which the hallucinating woman's glance tried to take refuge, all those things were transformed and became hostile towards her. And so the idea of chastisement and eternal punishment arose once more in her conscience and pressed upon her. She found herself in a nightmare brought about by her sin, crossing her arms on her breast to defend herself against the threats of demons, trying to say prayers while tongue-tied with terror, finally throwing herself upon the anchor of repentance, her ultimate salvation. She felt she was lost, and now from the depths of her heart she was asking for pity from the divine Spouse whom she had betrayed, from Jesus who was good and great, from Him who pardons.

Camilla's voice exhaled in sighs, was mixed with a tremulous rumbling, then was extinguished in slow and regular breathing, as gradually the excitement of her mystical dream died down. The shadows continued to flicker. The Crucified One was not yet descending from the wall to gather into his gentle arms the sheep that was coming back into the fold.

17

'The Lord has said through the mouth of Joel, son of Pethuel: "And it shall come to pass that I will pour out my Spirit upon all flesh; and your sons and your daughters shall prophesy; your old men shall dream dreams, your young men shall see visions."[17]

'This spirit of which the Apostles had the first fruits and the blessing, was for them and for us a Spirit of truth, a Spirit of Sanctity and a Spirit of strength... O divine love, O sacred bond which unites the Father and the Son, omnipotent Spirit, faithful comforter of the afflicted, penetrate into the depths of our hearts and pour into them your great light.'

That was how Don Gennaro Tierno, at Pentecost, preached from the high altar to the listening people. Above him, on high, the third person of the Sacred Trinity opened the radiant arch with wings of gold, and in the church the candles gave out a red light similar to the reflection of a fire. The enormous stone pillars supporting the two naves, covered with barbarian Christian sculpture, made their heavy way towards the altar; on the walls the remains of mosaics left spots of

37

dark colour; some heads of Apostles, some stiff arms of saints, some angels' wings still emerged from the darkening and peeling caused by the passage of time. Among the mosaics hung little ex-voto ships; a complete flotilla of sailing boats was there, dedicated to the temple by survivors of shipwrecks. And in the middle of all this rough, primordial solemnity spiralled up a group of slender pink columns supporting the pulpit, which was also marble, decorated with acanthus flowers, and enlivened with bas reliefs.

'Shed your sweet dew upon this desert land, so that its long aridity may cease. Send the celestial rays of your love into the sanctuaries of our souls, so that by penetrating there they may light the flame which will consume our weakness, our negligence, our spiritual weariness!' continued the priest, rising to the supreme height of his eloquence and his vocal power.

Giuliana listened nearby, completely absorbed. She had taken refuge in the house of the Lord, she had returned to the bridal bed; she wanted the Lord to purify her and receive her once more into the loving kindness of his great embrace. That sudden gleam of faith blinded her, made her almost forget all her previous faults. It seemed to her that suddenly all the stains on her soul had been wiped out and all the dross of earthly impurity had fallen away from her flesh. She had never approached the altar of God with a more profound thrill of hope; she had never heard the word of God with a more durable intoxication.

From the very moment in which the horror of damnation had come into her mind, she had shut herself up in a sort of gloomy concentration; one might almost say she was supervising herself, supervising her own actions, her own thoughts, her slightest inclinations, through the fear which that vehement repentance instilled, through the anxiety to preserve intact within herself that flower of faith which had suddenly blossomed once more. It was a kind of assumption towards Jesus; it was a kind of jealous isolation from the life around, a repudiation of every human bond.

She was lifted up by the reading of sacred books; she threw herself into the contemplation of the images and mysteries; she fought against the tender baseness of the flesh, against the heat in the daytime, against the snares of the night, against the scents brought to her by the wind, against the breath which rose from her impure memories, against the voices which seemed to titillate her hearing and whisper to her of new secret pleasures.

After that solitary week of passion, she now placed her sacrifice at the foot of the altar: she drank in the balsam of the word of God, fixing her gaze high up on the radiant dove, and feeling herself gradually sinking in an ocean of ecstasy.

'Come then, come, sweet comforter of desolate souls, refuge in dangers, protector in calamity. Come, O you who purify souls from every stain and heal their wounds. Come, strength of the weak, support of those who fall. Come, guiding star of sailors, hope of the poor, salvation of those about to die,' continued Don Gennaro Tierno, tall in his silver chasuble, red-faced, with eyes bulging out of their sockets, with gestures that seemed to touch the sky.

In the church a sultry heat had thickened around the Christians. The naves were squashed against the pillars; in one window the head of St Luke the Evangelist, struck by the sun, sent out rays, and his great cloak formed an area of green twilight in the air. In that insubstantial light the marble pulpit rose up like a miraculous mystical flower.

'Come, O Spirit, come and take pity on us!…'

Giuliana held her eyes up; on the wave of all those invocations she ascended towards the saint's halo, penetrated by that ineffable sweetness which attracts the soul to the scent of spiritual aromas. For one instant she thought she saw the golden dove flash her a gleam of consent, and the heart in her breast leapt in rejoicing, like St John in the womb of Elizabeth at the visit of the Virgin Mary.

'Through our Lord Jesus Christ. Amen.'

The priest, all silvery, turned towards the ciborium, saying the creed in a low voice. Two white thurifers at the sides began to swing the smoking, fragrant thuribles. Giuliana, who was nearby, was enveloped in a cloud of incense, and all at once an unconquerable flood of nausea rose to her throat from the depths of her maternity and made her twist her mouth.

18

Was there then no escape? For a few more days she vacillated, waiting for the final proof. She felt dizzy when she got up, when she put her feet to the ground; a vague faintness attacked her in the evening, a weakness in which thought, will, memories seem to exist in the confusion, the wavering drowsiness of the small hours. She did things out of habit, with the gestures of a sleepwalker, with the slowness of a weary woman. In the schoolroom, if the scent of bread hot from the oven was borne on the wind, she felt she was dying, she felt as though all her insides were suddenly rising into her mouth: the taste of lye was on her tongue. One day, when one of the infants was sucking cherries, a violent desire for that fruit made her twist about in her seat, grow pale, and sweat. Then, after a meal, full of nausea, she lay full length on the bed, she let herself be overcome by drowsiness: the heat was heavy, the flies were buzzing, the cries of a seller of spectacles passed by beneath the window, hoarse in the silence.

She was too discouraged to go to church any more, and incense repelled her.

She did not think about Marcello any more; she did not see him any more, she had only an uncertain memory of him, as of a distant dream: she was completely obsessed with her present anxiety.

Lindoro came up bringing water, as before. He arrived red and dripping with sweat; he put the containers down, throwing sidelong glances at Giuliana. Giuliana withdrew into the other room, or bent over her work; inside her cheeks her teeth were feverishly clenched, only tiny movements betraying her repressed anger; her eyes clouded over.

Lindoro went away like a whipped cur; but the thought of having possessed that woman disturbed his blood: he would have liked to drag her away with him, be her master, own her like a commodity to use and sell. And so sensual greed and the greed for profit were mingled in him.

One day he was waiting at the door into the street for Camilla to go out; then he rushed upstairs to surprise Giuliana, to find her alone in the house. Giuliana recognised his knock at the door, and she became agitated.

'What do you want from me, what do you want?' she asked in a smothered voice, without opening the door.

'Listen to me a moment, listen to me! Don't be afraid; I won't do you any harm…'

'Go away, you wretch, you vile creature, you fiend…' the woman burst out, vehemently shrieking out abuse, letting fly with all the hatred she had built up against him. 'Go away, go away!'

And, exhausted, she retired into her room, and threw herself on the pillows, gnawing them as she wept. She was shaken all over by a violent tremor, and a convulsive stiffening of her jaws made her sobs sound painful.

19

There was no escape. Maria Camastra's daughter had drunk vitriol and so she was dead, with a child of three months in her womb. Clemenza Jorio's daughter had thrown herself off the bridge, and so she was dead, in the mud of the Pescarina. And so she, too, must die.

When this thought flashed into Giuliana's mind, the afternoon was fading. All the bells were ringing joyfully on the eve of Corpus Christi; huge crowds of swallows were squawking and whirling over the Brina Palace, assembling on the arch to chatter. A magnificent red cloud stood over the buildings, like that cloud perhaps which poured fire and brimstone down on the wickedness of Sodom.

That thought, as it flashed into her mind, bewildered Giuliana, and she was afraid. Then, bit by bit, as her feeling of shame persuaded her to take that step, a muffled vitality started to rebel deep within her, and she quaked inside. All at once she felt her shame and the heat of her blood blotching her forehead and her cheeks. She got up from her chair, twisting her arms in the agitation of the conflict. And at last, with an outburst of nervous strength, she went out of the room, went into the kitchen, and looked on the tables for a glass and the pack of sulphur matches. The strong smell of coal upset her stomach; her brain felt dizzy. She found everything; she put the matches to dissolve in the water; she went back into her room and hid the glass in one corner, beneath the furniture.

'My God! My God!'

She was afraid of being found like that, alone with the evidence of her intention. Suddenly the dead body of Cristina Jorio came back into her mind, glimpsed that day when they were carrying it to her mother's house on a stretcher: a body swollen like a wineskin, with mud in her hair, in the hollows of her eyes, in her mouth, between her violet toes…

'My God! My God, to die!'

And she started as though a cold, stiff hand had been placed on her head; a shudder ran through all her limbs, and stayed on her head momentarily with the impression of a blade that was cutting into it to slice the skin off; and she saw the horror and repulsiveness of it, with that whiteness which dilates the eye sockets.

'No, no, no!' she said in a changed voice, as if she wanted to drive away from herself the touch of something horrible. And she went to the window, and thrust out her head, seeking some refuge.

She remained there, rooted to the spot, stunned by that vision of biblical fire and by that coven of black birds. When she turned back into the room a little way, she caught sight of a strange gleam in the shadows, the glitter of the golden half-moons on the dress of the Madonna of Loreto and the glitter of the medals. She was still afraid; she pressed herself against the window-sill, she looked out further; she remained there, without having the courage to move. At that point, in her immobility, her evening weakness began to invade her, and she pressed her heavy head between her palms, and half closed her eyes.

'Ah!'

Suddenly she had a glimmer of hope. Yes, yes, she remembered! Spacone, the sorcerer, that old man with the long beard who performed miracles and had medicines for every illness… He had occasionally been in the district, astride a white mule, with two golden triangles at his ears, and wearing a row of large buttons like silver spoons without handles. Very many women came to the doors and called out to him, and blessed him. He had cured all sorts of illnesses with certain herbs and certain waters and certain signs made with his thumb and certain magic words. He must have remedies for that thing too… yes, yes, he must have them!

And with that gleam of hope Giuliana came to life again, while

42

her listlessness grew worse and worse. Everything was sinking into the dusk before her eyes; the scarlet day, penetrated by the ashes of the approaching night, was going, fading slowly into a colour between pink and violet, withdrawing gradually from the lower parts of the town, ending in a muting of contrasts. A swallow went by, like a bat, skimming her head. A flood of glowing summer vitality struck her in the face, bringing a feeling of suffocation and a sense of throbbing.

With an involuntary and unconscious movement, she put her hands on her womb and held them there an instant. Something like a vague maternal feeling flitted through her mind. And from the depths, by who knows what internal process, a memory of her distant convalescence awakened. Ah, it was in March... a great smiling whiteness... and onto her rained the seeds, the soft down.

20

And so it was that the next morning she left the house, stealthily; she made her way alone out of the district, taking the new road to Chieti.

Spacone lived in the vicinity of San Rocco. Under the aegis of a druidical oak he worked his miracles and formulated his oracular responses. The whole countryside, for twenty miles around, had recourse to him, as to an apostle of Providence. When there were epidemics among the local livestock, herds of oxen and horses were gathered round the oak to receive the talismans to preserve them from disease; the prints of equine and bovine hooves made what looked like a magic ring on what was merely grass on the ground.

As Giuliana made her way there, there was in the region of Pescara a great play of light and shadow. The nomadic clouds were migrating from the sea to the mountain, like caravans with their great loads of water, through that Arabian sky in the month of June. At intervals large areas of land were immersed in shade, other areas emerged into the light; and since the shade was dark blue and changeable, the countryside gave the appearance of a floating archipelago abounding in trees and wheat. The singing of so many birds and the ripeness of the crops made a joyful sight.

The moment she saw all this Giuliana had a feeling of solace: the freedom of the countryside, the pleasure of seeing the light on the foliage, the genial scents of the air around sent the blood coursing through her body, and as she saw the horizon spread out, her hope was more strongly renewed and she exulted. As always, she abandoned herself to external influences; she felt her anxiety lifting; only two feelings kept her going – her hope of physical salvation and her desire to reach her destination. Briefly, she imagined the beneficent Old Man at her destination rising up in a mysterious light. With her native tendency to superstition, she transformed that figure, magnifying it and clothing it in Christian sweetness, surrounding it with a halo. All the rumours which circulated among the common people then came confusedly back to her mind and threw splashes of miraculous light on Spacone's forehead. Then she remembered that Rosa Catena, in a far-off time of illness, had spoken of the Old Man with devout reverence, and had cited miracles. A blind man from Torre de' Passeri had gone to San Rocco and returned after three days with eyes that could see and a dark blue number on his forehead. A woman from Spoltore, who was possessed by an evil spirit, had come back as meek and mild as a lamb, after taking two sips of water from a little dry pumpkin.

So bit by bit, along the road, with the combination of so many scattered elements, a kind of legend had formed in Giuliana's mind. And bit by bit, since mankind can do nothing without the help of God, she was persuaded that the old man was someone sent from heaven, a redeemer of souls from their physical bondage, a distributor of heavenly grace on earth to those who had fallen. Had not hope ultimately and suddenly descended on the sinner, as if by divine influence, by means of those signs kindled in the air? And at Pentecost had not the dove sent down from on high, in the eyes of those who were praying, a lightning flash of promise?

That promise was now being kept on the holy day of Corpus Christi. And so Giuliana, warmed by her faith and her rejoicing, walked on the dust of the new road, unbothered by the effort of walking. The hedges on both sides were whitened as if by birds' excrement. Groups of sounding poplars stood at the edge of the road; and their trunks, like large pieces of old silver, reflected the variations in the light. Peasants from Villa del Fuoco – dwarfish women with snub noses and thick lips, Kafirs with white skins – were coming the other way in twos and threes. Around, in the immense theatre of the countryside, the giant vicissitudes of the clouds were being acted out.

Giuliana went past the mill and the villa: nervous energy quickened her steps. She felt the wind beating on the nape of her neck, and at intervals she heard the poplars rustling overhead. But the flickering of the shadows and the dust began to obscure her sight a little; the heat of the movement went to her head; her will was entirely occupied by the unaccustomed effort needed to proceed. She went on like this in a sort of growing stupefaction which became a feeling of discomfort; and, overcome by the effort and the heat, she let herself be tempted by a mass of olive trees climbing up on her left.

Four or five gypsies passed along – half naked, bronzed, with a sort of shine on their breasts, astride great reddish asses. One of them was whistling while he dug his heels into the belly of his mount. All had sticks in their hands and carried leather haversacks at their sides. They looked at the woman who had taken refuge under the olives and murmured a few words and laughed.

Giuliana was fearful of those eyes whose whites showed up so clearly, and remained in a state of bewilderment until the group had passed into the distance. She began to feel discouraged; she began to feel worried at being alone, because a premonition of rain was shuddering over the countryside, and a solemn silence came down through the air from the gathering clouds. She was leaning against a tree trunk; at times she was assailed by cool gusts of wind which froze the sweat in her pores, gusts of wind which rushed towards her with the rustling tread of an animal on the grass; meanwhile, all around, the flickering of the sun was like the echo of water breaking or rather like the reflection of a distant meteor. Many flowers of a pale, sulphurous yellow were rippling at the foot of the olive trees.

Then those good trees brought a memory back into the woman's mind. All the church was full of blessed palms and aromas that day; and she was walking among the people, leaning on Marcello's arm, very happily... But, as she lingered on that thought, her memory became confused; everything fled away from her with the uncertainty of a dream. All that was left was the dull beating of her heart and the gasps of anxiety which made it hard to breathe. She now had the stupid sensation of sleep falling on her brain with the weight of a mallet-blow on the forehead of an ox. She had enough will-power left to give herself a feeble shake and go down to the road.

The clouds which had gathered in the direction of Majella had taken on the diaphanous grey colour of a hanging mass of water. Huge whirlwinds, even more heavily laden, were approaching from the seashore; and in addition some florid intervals of indigo were spreading on high. A damp smell was already rising from the dust, rising from the countryside panting in anticipation. The unmoving trees seemed to absorb the light, rising blackened in the smoky air, populating the distance with vague shapes.

Giuliana was walking with an immense effort, and she felt her strength was about to abandon her.

'What I'll do,' she thought, 'is get to that tree and then fall down.'

But she did not fall down. On her right she could make out the houses of San Rocco. A peasant came running towards her.

'Is that San Rocco?'

'Yes, yes, turn at the first byway.'

Large drops began to splash down; then suddenly the rain grew heavier and the air was streaming with long white arrows, long whips that cracked as they struck. Then the clouds were shaken into a monstrous commotion: splashing rays erupted on this side and on that. All the hills in the background, seen through the bands of rain, lit up for an instant and were then extinguished again. A feeble silver peacefulness ascended the Majella, in a region of mist.

Giuliana tried to run towards the oak, a rifle-shot away. The rain-drops beat on the nape of her neck, ran down her spine, struck her face; and she was already soaked to the skin. She could not take a step on the slippery ground; she fell and got up again, twice. Then, almost crazy, she tried to shout out in the direction of a house.

'Help! Help!'

A woman came out to hold her up, followed by two barking dogs.

Giuliana automatically let herself be led, without managing to get a word out between her clenched teeth. She was livid and her face was contorted. Despite the questions which her hostess put to her, it was some time before she gathered herself together. And then, suddenly, hearing Spacone's name, she remembered everything.

'Ah, where is Spacone?' she asked.

'He's in Popoli, good lady; they've sent for him.'

Giuliana could not hold out any longer: she started to sob and tear her hair out.

'What do you want, good lady? What do you want? I'm his wife; I'm here…' whined the witch, holding onto her wrists and encouraging her to speak.

Giuliana hesitated for a moment, then she told her everything in a rush, between sobs, covering her face.

'Wait. There is a remedy; but it costs fifty *soldi*, good lady,' said the witch, in that idiom full of soft vowels, singing the beautiful appellation as a refrain.

Giuliana undid a knot in her handkerchief and offered five little silver coins. Then she waited more calmly.

The room was vast, but low. The walls, covered with saltpetre, were something of the colour of dried snakeskin, and looked like the scales of reptiles. Rough Christian idols in maiolica populated that ancient house; strange shapes of tools and instruments cluttered up the tables. The whole impression was of somewhere religious, a sanctuary looked after by a simple monk.

Spacone's wife, in front of the fireplace, was making up her philtre, in silence. She was a tall, bony woman, with a white face, with a misshapen nose the violet colour of certain southern figs, with red hair that was smooth on her temples, with two little albinotic eyes, and tattoos on her chin, her forehead, and the backs of her hands.

Giuliana downed the liquid at one gulp; but she felt, immediately afterwards, a terrible bitterness eating away at her palate and insides. She remained with her mouth open, pressing her hands on her stomach, with one foot tapping rapidly on the floor, in the pang of the first uterine contraction.

'Now, good lady! Bear up!' the witch repeated to her, fixing her with those two whitish mollusc-like eyes, rubbing her loins gently. 'You've time to get to Pescara… Hurry up! Hurry up!'

Giuliana could not respond: all she could utter were cries. Cramps were tightening her stomach, stiffening her respiratory muscles, making her want to vomit. Her eyeballs rolled up, as though she were showing the first symptoms of an epileptic fit. The excessive strength of the drink had unexpected effects on her feeble constitution. The false labour came suddenly, with one of those terrible haemorrhages by which life slips away gently, insensibly.

'Jesus, Jesus, Jesus!' murmured the witch, disquieted, suddenly afraid in front of Giuliana's supine body stirred only by certain little convulsive undulations. 'Jesus, help me!'

At her entreaties Giuliana recovered. And when after some time the discharge seemed to have stopped, Giuliana was able to get onto her feet; she managed to go out, pushed by the woman; she managed to reach the new road, staggering, as pale as if no drop of blood remained in her veins, but kept alive by the hope that the greatest danger was now over.

By now the countryside was all fresh and bright. A line of carts passed by, laden with chalk; the burly carters from Letto Manopello, full of wine, were stretched out on the sacks, smoking. When Giuliana was behind the line, one of them, the last one, shouted out.

'Hoy, do you want a lift, darling?'

Automatically Giuliana let herself be pulled up by the man's strong arms, and she sat on the sacks. She did not hear the coarse laughter and the obscene jokes which were passed on from cart to cart.

With involuntary, instinctive energy she held her knees pressed together to impede the flow of blood. Gradually she felt her mind filled with a sort of numbness, so that the frequent bumping of the wheels on the gravel gave her only a dull ache and the stench of the pipes only slightly disturbed her sense of smell. But by now the distant murmur in her ears, the glare in her eyes, and her dizziness showed that she was losing blood from her brain. Several times she would have fallen if she had not been supported by the arms of the carter who, encouraged by her silent docility, made some coarse attempt to caress her.

The town of Pescara appeared at the brow of the road in full sunlight, and its sounds were carried on the wind.

'They're going in procession,' said one of the men. All the others used their whips, and the road resounded to the heavy trotting, the ringing bells, and the crack of the whips.

The violent jolts and the noise brought Giuliana back for a moment to a sense of the reality around her. But, because the man had one arm round her waist and was breathing fumes of wine on her cheek, she was blindly impelled to shout and gesticulate as if she were delirious. And the spectre of Lindoro rose up suddenly in front of her clouded eyes and was able even to raise horror and repugnance in what little sensibility remained in her nerves. As soon as the cart stopped, she slid from the sacks onto the ground, and tried to move her legs, with the anxious frenzy of someone trying to reach a place in which it would be safe to fall down.

Along the road the little maidens were coming towards her, veiled in white, with coloured candles in their hands, and singing. Behind this angelic host a great fluttering of flags and baldachins filled the air which was freshened by the recent rain. And they were singing:

'*Tantum ergo sacramentum*
Veneremur cernui…'[18]

Giuliana, realising what was about to happen, turned into the alley; she got to Rosa Catena's house and went in; taken dizzy, she fell in the middle of the floor. And, as the flow of blood recommenced, the lower part of her body was paralysed, and all her powers of voluntary movement were spent.

Rosa was not at home: the procession had attracted the whole district that day. In one corner of the room Muà, Rosa's father, a prodigy of human old age, deformed and confined to a wooden chair for years by arthritis, poked the tiles around him vaguely with the end of his stick to discover the reason for the sudden noise.

Then, in a pool of blood, Giuliana was struck by a paroxysm of convulsions. The contractions of her muscles threw her torso about here and there; her limbs stretched out with the impulsive palpitation of the leg of a fatally wounded animal; she clenched her fists, opened them again, and then closed them again; her eyeballs retreated into their sockets, under the violet eyelids, with a movement like that of a flower which retracts its limp petals. All of a sudden, her head turned right round, under the last blow of nervous apoplexy; her bloodless trunk went rigid in paralysis. A light tremor appeared in the sinews of her neck, and, after a moment, her clenched fingers relaxed.

Muà, without understanding, felt around himself with his stick, in vain, mumbling with his toothless mouth.

A Sentimental Tale

1

Galatea lifted those cold yellowish eyes of hers from the papers, raising herself up from her long slender waist, making her thin white fingers crackle.

'I've finished.'

'Thank you, Galatea. Are you tired?' murmured Cesare in that hoarse voice of his, continuing to turn the pages of a large book on the reading desk.

'A little. I'll have a rest.'

So she let herself sink into the silence; her ashen head of hair rested comfortably against the background of the dark leather of the chair-back, and a shadow softened the bright marble of her face. Around her the library seemed to be enjoying the sound, peaceful sleep of an old man; it breathed of parchment and ancient walnut, and dust whirled round in the shafts of sunlight.

For quite a while Cesare and Galatea had been spending their time like this, studying, in an august, monastic quiet. He had come to his maternal uncle's villa to find solitude, sacrificing his blooming youth, his loves; gradually all the exuberance, all the restlessness of his nature had settled down into a profound, virile serenity, had clarified into a happy clairvoyance; the worship of art was gradually infusing something spiritual and sacerdotal even into his appearance. It was a slow process, brought about by habit, by that soft light in which he lived, by that twilight where his myopic eyes were almost always dim, where the blood in his face was growing pale.

Galatea was a reserved and thoughtful companion for him, a helper, a courteous amanuensis who never got lost among the labyrinths and arabesques of learned writings. She grew up to be like the stalk of a flower, she grew up in the profound melancholy of that house where she had never seen her mother smile… Her poor dead mother! With what a long sigh of love and grief did Galatea look at the veil spread over the portrait of her poor dead mother! That portrait was in a large empty room, on a white wall, there, at the far end of the villa; no sound reached there, feeble light came sadly through the curtains. When Galatea crossed the threshold, a cold trickle of terror ran through her, repugnance creaked through her bones; she felt as if she were going underground; all that whiteness gave her a sensation of immensity. Nevertheless, she stayed there for a long time, on her knees, praying, praying, while the edge of the veil fluttered at every breath of wind on that image of a corpse; her bewildered eyes continued to look into vacancy, and in that vacancy her prayer was lost in the weak murmur of her lips. Slowly the daylight began to fade. Then in the twilight the fluttering seemed to grow larger, to become gigantic; gradually an enormous piece of the shroud spread through the room with a gust of corruption. She shuddered at its contact; she was frozen and as still as stone, she stayed there until they dragged her out, quite pale, trembling all over.

But she went back to that dark and solitary adoration, she went back to it with a gush of tears, calling out on the dead woman through her sobs. She wanted to see her, to see her once, but alive, but with life in her eyes, see her beautiful and laughing, once only!

'She was blonde, wasn't she? As blonde as I am, wasn't she?' she asked her father, raising her moist eyes, trying to flash a smile through her tears of affection.

So she had grown up, in grief. She was rather like those white plants, which have lived in the dark, which seem to be engendered from a diseased human body, and shade sepulchres with their sadness. The great sun, the great light irritated her: she half closed her eyes, defending those poor weak eyes from harm. And yet she loved flowers. Behind the villa, in a piece of ground, some sickly and rich vegetation drowsed in the shade; there were large, fleshy leaves, brown shading into violet, covered with down, like mould; there were dwarf branches, naked, like dead reptiles or enormous grubs; there were flat blades of pale green, lined with white, and spotted like the backs of frogs. Certain big purple flowers opened like goblets, rose from the earth on long tubes, without any foliage; certain calyxes, as rosy as human skin, swelled on their twisted stalks; certain dark scarlet mouths emitted stamens like small yellowish tongues. Their petals were slimy, like fungus, the sheaths inside them were waxen honeycombs. Some tulips opened lazily in a shaft of sunlight; some peonies triumphed with huge flowers of deep carmine; and around, in autumn, the clematis seemed a tangle of hairy spiders or bunches of greyish plumes. Only the elder emitted perfume, fresh and mild, from within its broad white inflorescences. Butterflies swept past; groups of snails went here and there, stealing among the juicy plants, leaving shining trails.

Galatea loved that place: that sad vegetable rabble held an enchantment for her; like her they suffered, like her they were weak. As she stood upright in the middle of them, in her dark dress, she looked like a tall solitary flower. She had a sickly feeling of tenderness for those poor existences which were languishing without a glance from the sun; she collapsed, heard a groan rise up, heard the groan of dying things. Into her constitution, full of watery humour, a mysterious sense of death had seemed to flow since the day of her birth, which was also her mother's final day.

2

That was how she was living when Cesare arrived. At the beginning she had a feeling almost of disgust; it seemed to her that this young man was coming to disturb the deep, mild calmness of the house, coming to interrupt the silent melancholy in which she wanted to settle, where she believed she could feel the invisible presence of the dead woman. But gradually he conquered that disgust, he was kind and courteous. He was slowly overcome by the silence, by the deep concentration of everything around him; and he was absorbed in art.

They spent hours in the old Count's library. Light came into the great rectangular hall through the opaque panes of the great windows, setting off the ornaments of dull gold on the walnut bookshelves, and getting lost in the corners. The noble armorial bearings of carved wood crowned the ceiling; and in the centre of the hollow vault the broad flourishes of a seventeenth-century fresco glowed red with a background of yellowish clouds. In half-light the rows of books seemed like a wall covered in cracks, green here and there with moss, splashed by the rain, streaked by snails.

Galatea read or transcribed; or she listened to Cesare speaking, with cold, wide-open eyes, relaxing on the leather chair. Even amid the fragrant, blooming eclogues of Virgil, and the winged, plaintive lyrics of the *dolce stil novo*, their idyll did not blossom.[19]

Galatea smiled only in an austere and virginal way, like an ancient vestal; she wished to belong completely to her sad household god, who was watching her from behind the funerary veil.

And only once did Cesare feel his artistic constitution quiver in her presence. It was a hot afternoon in June, but the library was silent, immersed in its bluish coolness, with the curtains drawn across the windows.

He entered; the girl was sleeping peacefully in the rich flowing folds of a long straight dress, with her head leaning on the big celestial globe. The globe seemed to be made of yellowed ivory, it looked like a huge human skull around which strange figures of animals were whirling; Galatea's loose hair fell with subtle reflections down onto her shoulders; it covered her cheeks; and a golden band of sunlight going through the coolness lit up above her head a row of books in parchment that was greenish like oxidised copper. She had her arms around the globe; her broad sleeves revealed her white, diaphanous flesh with its network of veins.

Cesare was looking at her, thinking of the Scandinavian Norns and Merovingian maidens, when she awakened as the sun struck her and smiled at him with her lively eyes in which for an instant the new light and torpor and wonder struggled with each other.

'Why do you awaken, Galatea? You are so beautiful when you are asleep!' he said ingenuously in his admiration.

She was still smiling, tying her hair up; her right cheek was suffused with scarlet from the pressure of the globe.

But that germ of an idyll remained shut in a sonnet, for ever, like a flower or a butterfly in its bright prison of amber.

3

One day the Count, before dinner, announced the arrival of the Baroness de Rosa, second wife of his brother Federico, veteran of summer triumphs in Rimini and Livorno. He showed Cesare a letter written on blue paper with a golden crest.

'Read this,' he said.

Cesare took it; and the sharp scent that came from the sheet of paper disturbed him strangely, almost gave him a feeling of disquiet. Across the paper rose a flight of little white storks, and among the storks the little nervous characters followed one another in violet, exquisitely.

'When does she arrive?' asked Galatea.

'Tomorrow.'

She did indeed come. She was a very young aunt, a splendid Andalusian figure with very dark eyes full of desire and mystery.

'Oh, my fair-haired beauty! Oh, my beautiful fair-haired little doll!' she exclaimed, enfolding Galatea in her arms, ruffling her hair at the front, tormenting her with kisses.

'And you, Cesare? You too are still here, in the lonely castle, a page, a troubadour, a knight... what?'

And she laughed with little tinklings of crystal and vibrating metals, throwing her head back, while her pink gums were revealed rather cruelly and her bosom shook beneath its satin breastplate.

'Aren't you afraid of having a spell cast on you, Cesare?'

That was how she was; she spoke with a saucy, prattling volubility, with an adorable, sparkling impediment on the letter 'r'. The fresh wave of her voice seemed to break and ripple against the letter 'r'.

'Always here, always here, Galatea? Will you never want to break the magic circle then? I shall snatch her away from you, Count, I shall snatch away this Jolanda[20] of yours with the pensive eyes... But you really do have two emeralds for eyes, Galatea! Why are you looking at me like that? Do you like me?...'

And she impatiently took off the long black chamois-leather gloves which enclosed her arms right up to the elbows.

'Let's go. Lead on.'

That sudden outburst of happiness awakened echoes in the hall, the vaulted roof quivered with gloomy sonority; as Vinca rustled away on the ancient mosaic floors she left perfume in her wake, through all the rooms full of carved wood and florid carpets.

Beside that woman, Galatea was at first almost stunned; then she was filled with something like a dull irritation by that nervous instability, those sharp waves of scent which nauseated her, those bursts of laughter which struck her eardrums sharply. She wanted to rebel against frenzied kisses, vivacious caresses, affected flatteries.

'A beautiful doll!' Vinca often murmured this, with clenched teeth, her lips apart, with a touch of feline tenderness, as she pressed the girl's forehead between her palms and drew it towards her mouth.

'No, please don't call me that, Aunt, I beg you,' Galatea ejaculated once, with a faint tremor of anger in her voice.

'Beautiful doll!' repeated Vinca. She cast into the air one of those bursts of fresh laughter, like a peal of bells, throwing herself back onto the divan, in a provocative pose. On the divan the sun, coming in through the window, reddened once more the floral patterns of faded silk on the old silver fabric; and against that background her beautiful woman's figure, sheathed in its cashmere dress, stood out, surrounded by the motes in the sunbeams. It was a picture in delicate colours; on the wall hung a faded arras on which two knights were pursuing a fugitive stag. Vinca was laughing; her laughter seemed to shine in the sunlight. When Cesare appeared on the threshold:

'Enter, Doctor, enter!' exclaimed the aunt, rising and holding out her hand to the young man. 'Calm Galatea down, for goodness' sake!'

But now the girl was giving a thin smile. Cesare had involuntarily breathed in the delicate perfume of violets which stole through the air, the same perfume as there had been on the letters with the storks; his nostrils were quivering with pleasure. He was coming from the heavy musty smell of the worm-eaten volumes, from the silence of the library which Vinca's appealing laughter had reached. It had reached into the silence, while he, bent over the pages, felt the healthy joyfulness of the goliardic songs rise from the pages, rushing with a lively thunder of Latin rhymes in the flying cadence.

O! O! Totus floreo.[21]

He had pricked up his ears; and for one instant the bursts of laughter pealed in his ears with the cock-a-doodle-doo of a mad stanza.

Veni, veni, venias,
Ne me mori facias,
Hyria hysria nazaza
Trilliriuo.[22]

All the ardour and desire of youth seemed to reawaken suddenly in his blood like the music of battle and victory, and regerminate with fresh violence. He seemed to feel through all his limbs something like a rustling of broken shells and bursting buds, under the happy hail of those bursts of laughter and those refrains.

O! O! Totus floreo.

He leapt to his feet. He found that cold solitude oppressive; he hated it, that solitude…

'Enter, Doctor, enter,' said the crystalline voice of the Baroness.

With what felicitous audacity the Baroness' torso stood out against the old whitish background and its red flowers! From the delicate lobes of her ears the silver rings hung gypsy-fashion in contrast with the dark complexion of the cheeks; and a light down adorned her cheeks, shading even her upper lip, very lightly.

'Listen, Galatea, my little girl; let's make peace,' she murmured in a submissive and caressing tone of voice. 'Let's go down, into the avenue; let's go into the sun with Cesare… Do you want to come?'

'No, Aunt; leave me here. *I* can't go into the sun,' replied Galatea meekly.

'Are you coming, Cesare?' Vinca asked the young man.

Bowing, Cesare offered her his arm.

4

They walked along the avenue of locust trees, alone. Around the couple there was a soft fluttering of leaves, and the smell of dead flowers from limp clusters, an indistinct smell, in the growing melancholy.

The time of year did not trouble Vinca's soul: she went along humming an arietta by Suppè[23], with a certain bold nodding of the head.

'My goodness, say something: recite verses to me, sing me madrigals even,' she finally burst out. 'But do talk about something! Oh, do you want us to listen to the lamentation of the dying leaves and the evening voices and the simpering Hail Marys, and sigh? Ah!…'

And she sighed with adorable grace, lifting the whites of her eyes to heaven.

'No, no, Signora,' said Cesare, laughing; and as he laughed he showed his gleaming rows of regular teeth, under his brown moustache. He was not ugly: there was a pleasant pallor on his face, which meant that the irregular lines of the face were softened. Against that pallor, his clear, myopic eyes, almost always half closed, at times dilated immeasurably and the irises, overwhelmed by the pupils, looked at times like two black holes.

'No, no, Aunt,' he repeated, in a tiny voice.

'What is that smell, nephew?'

'I can perceive the scent of violets,' said Cesare in a melodious, gentle voice.

Their laughter rang out heartily under the serene vault of vegetation.

'Ah, nephew, have you just composed the first line of a sonnet or the beginning of a declaration? What boldness and ingenuity! You're starting to make me tremble. Stand aside.'

And she tried to free herself from his arm, with an air of mockery and fear; but Cesare held her imprisoned in his grasp.

'Stay with me, Aunt. I am innocent.'

They were acting like this in fun. But Cesare, when he took hold of her bare hand to detain her, felt a gentle shiver go right through his bones; and he looked at that little hand with the long fingers and onyx nails, which had a deep letter 'm' on the palm. From the wrist, beneath the bracelets of gold and nielloed silver, some greenish veins branched out, to be lost in the mystery of the cashmere dress, like the threads of copper in a piece of alabaster.

'Stay with me, Aunt.'

They were in front of a large, solitary basin. On the stagnant waters floated yellowish splashes of putrefaction, and some pale red, leathery leaves extended in masses almost up to the grassy rim. In the centre a group of fishtailed tritons watched over that silence which had not been broken by the showering jets for a long time; moss and lichen formed a sort of striped cloak on the old stone; at the base green filaments of stonecrop were spreading.

'Let's sit down here,' said Cesare, uncovering a section of coarse bas-relief which had fallen down into the grass. He felt uneasy, while Vinca sat down and looked at him with her lively eyes full of pity.

'Here, at my feet, O Cesare!' she ordered, in a jokingly imperious voice.

'No, never.'

'Here, at my feet,' she repeated.

'Here I am, Vinca; you win.'

They were acting like this in fun. But Cesare's head almost touched her knees; and she could see the young man's white nape, the nape of Antinous, exquisitely fashioned.

'Look, Cesare. They look like butterflies as they fall.'

She pointed to the leaves raining one by one onto the waters; she wanted to speak, she was starting to be afraid of the silence, she was gradually starting to lose her wittiness. That was the only remark she could think of, commonplace and sentimental in that place, at that moment.

'Look…'

She gently repulsed Cesare's timid attempts at caresses, his unsteady fingers on the ribbons of her dress; and that timidity seduced her. Cesare was not looking at the leaves, because one of her tiny shoes was twinkling in the grass, and on that iridescent leather he could see the small movements which Vinca was making at times with the toes of her narrow foot. And his face turned paler when, as he crumpled one of the ribbons, his fingers bumped against one of her knees.

'It's late; let's go,' said the lady, rising. Her voice shook.

But then she felt her legs embraced by Cesare's arms. He had remained prostrate like a slave and was holding up his deathly pale face where an attempt at a laugh was struggling with a shudder of desire.

'Traitor!' she murmured, bending pliantly towards his mouth.

5

They returned.

'So soon?' said Galatea, with a cruelly ironic note in her voice, gazing at them with cold, prophetic eyes.

That day, for the first time, she had not prayed to the household god! As soon as Vinca's peals of laughter faded away down the stairs and the couple's steps on the sand of the avenue had grown faint, she was invaded by a feeling of gloomy anxiety, a gloomy dismay weighed on her. It was an unexpected assault, against which she felt herself weak, against which she felt herself defenceless; it was like the sudden blazing up of a fire which she had carried within herself, for a long time, unconsciously. At first she did not believe, did not want to believe, did not wish to penetrate that new feeling that was overwhelming her and taking her over completely; she tried to relax, without suffering, in blind abandon.

But no; her heart, from the depths of her soul, Cesare's image issued, victoriously. Was it true, then? Did she love him, then? Would she then be unfaithful to her poor dead mother?

'Oh, Mamma! Oh, Mamma!' she sighed brokenly, twisting her arms, hiding among the cushions her face which was burning with tears.

Gradually that pain receded; a more human passion arose, a more human torment arose. Vinca's laughter still seemed to ring through the hollow sonority of the vault. Vinca was there in front of her, stretched in abandonment on that divan, all perfumed and bright. Cesare was enveloping her completely with his greedy gaze: he had never had such a light in his eyes, never. They had walked alone, in the avenue, down there, under the trees, alone.

She was tormenting herself, as she waited.

'Poor Galatea, how bored you must have been!' said Vinca, stroking her hair, insinuating into her locks those fingers adorned with rings. 'But you're burning, Galatea… Feel, Count; she is feverish.'

'No, there's nothing wrong with me, Papa; nothing.'

She held her eyes fixed on Cesare, her eyes blazing in the deathly pallor of her face. Then she passed one hand across her brow; she felt a weariness, a weakening, through her whole body – a stealthy feeling of cold.

'I'm so sleepy; my head's so heavy… But I'm not feverish, no! I feel that I could sleep so very long,' she murmured, half closing her eyes slowly and wearily, as if she were ceasing to breathe. 'I could sleep… so… long…'

She fell back on her chair; an irresistible drowsiness spread through her poor exhausted veins, troubling her life.

'Galatea! Galatea!'

A wail came from her white lips in a gust.

'Galatea!'

6

Her lethargy lasted a long time. When she opened her eyes, where a cloud of lethargy still floated, she saw her father's bald head bending over her in a silent attitude of dread and grief.

'Where is Cesare?' she asked him, and her voice died in her throat.

'Over there, my daughter; with Vinca…'

She closed her eyes again, as if to weaken the intensity of the pang; she seemed to hear the faint sound of suffocated laughter.

Vinca and Cesare filled the whole of the old, austere house with their feelings of love; the secret of their love was hidden in the shade of the faded arrases where in the silk's roseate clarity a beautiful naked race of nymphs and huntresses had once flourished. Cesare abandoned himself to the embrace of that pleasure with all the impetuosity of a repressed nature; he could always see her before him, that beautiful and perverse charmer who always revealed her red gums when she laughed or smiled; he saw her arise among the enormous candelabra of carved walnut, among the big escutcheoned chairs, among the clouded, spotted mirrors, under the baldachins striped with gold, under the heavy doors, in the midst of all those dead things, everywhere, upright and bold and challenging.

Galatea sensed that new yearning; she had guessed it with the amazing instinct that had made her ill.

'Make me die! Make me die!' she repeated between her sobs, lying in a sad state in front of her mother's image, gazing with anguished eyes at that silent veil, down there, in the distant room. 'Make me die!'

But eventually Vinca left: her husband wanted her. It was a sudden parting, on a cold, grey October morning.

'Goodbye, Galatea. Goodbye, Count. Goodbye, Cesare.'

She was not sad; she was just rather pallid, behind her black veil. She kissed Galatea many times; she stretched out her hand to Cesare, who stood there without speaking.

'We'll see each other again in spring,' she cried out once more, bringing her face up to the window of the carriage, waving her fingers. And the trotting of the horses faded away along the avenue, under the locust trees drooping in the cloudy moisture.

Then Galatea felt a pleasant relief gradually penetrate into her soul; she felt the old silence descending again slowly and solemnly to reign over the house; together with the relief, she felt also a peaceful weariness in which her poor life was fading away as though it were being overwhelmed. They were the clear, warm days of an Indian summer: a veil of drowsiness fluttered over the countryside rejoicing in those last embraces of the sun.

She now loved the sun; she wanted its benign rays to envelop her like a flowing golden dress; she exposed her face to its full heat, closing her eyes, with a feeling of pleasure in her throat at its blandishments.

'How kind it is!' she said softly. Cesare, beside her, was looking at her with a smile full of melancholy.

'Cesare…' she burst out one day eventually, on an impulse, holding out to him her gaunt arms. But then she fell silent; she fell back again into that mute weariness from which she was trying in vain to escape. Her feeble breast breathed hoarsely beneath the folds of her dress.

She went up to the organ, which had remained unused for a long time in a corner of the library. Cesare worked the dusty bellows: the bellows panted with the deep breath of a human giant, in the silence, lifting the souls of the sounds into the long metallic pipes. On the keys Galatea recalled a harmony by Bach, uncertainly.

Into the library, through big open windows, came lively areas of light. The rows of books, at the unwonted irruption, revived, and they too threw their weak notes from their curved, worm-eaten backs. There was a whole range of colours: the *Annals* of Baronio and Raynaldo in greenish parchment took on uncertain reflections of ancient bronze; the *Acta Sanctorum* went yellow and white with a tint of Dominican habits, occupying almost the whole of a very high shelf; in that whiteness Strykius made a vivid spot of blue and the to brandish a bold splash of scarlet. Then there were the various dull tones of worn-out tapestries; then there were bits of old leather stuff, stains red as rust, of a livid violet, of a faded orange. But the sun enlivened those tones, raised new sparkles in the dead gold, infused an air of youth into those pages covered with the dust and mould of so many decades.

From the reeds of the organ the harmonies of Bach spread out timidly into the void; the keys scarcely yielded beneath Galatea's diaphanous fingers. She sensed the sonorous throbbing running through her nerves with a feeling almost of pain; she felt her breath coming short.

'Cesare,' she murmured in a small voice, letting herself go against the back of the chair, conquered by the fatal drowsiness of that room itself.

And, as she held out her arms, her gentle little soul finally breathed its last in a sigh.

In Lanciotto's Absence

1

'Oh, Donna Clara, how are you keeping?'

She smiled sadly at this greeting, because she felt her health was gradually abandoning her, perhaps for ever.

She tried to stay on her feet, to keep that great bony body on its feet despite its growing weakness: she looked so strong, despite her dense network of wrinkles, despite being tinted with the snow of old age. And then the allurements of spring were beginning, so pleasant in the countryside where she had lived for so many years; then that welcome, expected warmth was coming, which would make her better, which would certainly save her. All that she needed was the strength not to give in to that weariness, all that she needed was not to lose heart, all that she needed was to get some fresh air into her lungs to send her blood coursing. This confidence revived her spirits, made her almost merry, made her love the infantile noise with which Eva was cheering the room up, made her love the bursts of singing with which her daughter-in-law filled the rooms. That scent of human youthfulness which was rising all around, and the benevolence of that season which was coming to birth excited her, gave her the sort of momentary energy which certain liquors give, the boisterous upsurge of life which a sick person has on hearing a snatch of happy music. There was however something bitter in all this, the harshness which comes inevitably after every struggle. When her daughter-in-law, seeing how pale she was in the shaft of sunlight which came through the window-panes, stopped singing, feeling suddenly that pitying respect which healthy people feel for those who are suffering, and asked her if she really felt better, Donna Clara replied:

'Yes, Francesca, I feel well. Do go on singing.'

But the hoarse tone of her voice revealed some repressed irritation; and Francesca noticed that.

'Would you like me to get your bed ready, Mamma?'

'No, no.'

'Do you need anything?'

'No, really, nothing…'

Her impatience burst out. She would open the large windows and rest her elbows on the window-ledge, trying to take deep breaths of the health-giving air. Or she would call Eva over to her, and her little niece would throw herself at her with the blind frenzy of a child enraptured with all the hubbub, her flushed face laughing under its abundance of blond hair.

'Oh, Grandma!' cried the toddler, careless of the pain which the shock of the encounter caused to the old woman's knees. She stayed resting there, while Donna Clara enjoyed running her aristocratically long fingers through that thick head of vital hair which gave off the natural scent of infancy, like a health-giving bathe. For a moment that increase of tenderness did her good, and for a moment she felt, from that little body still shaking after its previous movement, the repercussion in herself of a sensation of unconscious joy; or rather, she felt that in that little body some part of her own being was alive, passed on by heredity, and she took pleasure in that. She raised her head from the toddler; she wanted to look into those pure, deep eyes, which seemed to be always opening wider in wonder.

'She has Valerio's eyes and forehead, hasn't she, Francesca?'

'Yes, Mamma; or rather, your eyes and your forehead.'

Then the wrinkles on Donna Clara's face gathered into rays of light, in the brightness of her gratified smile.

Then, when Eva, seized with a new burst of movement, darted away from her caresses, Donna Clara was left in a sort of stupefaction, like someone who feels she is losing a pleasant stimulant in one part of her limbs, and is afraid that, if she stirs, the very last wave of pleasure will vanish. Gradually the effort of combating her listlessness became painful, and gradually her obstinate resistance yielded; and a first vague disquiet which was rapidly turning into fear, and then into real terror – the terror of someone who has exhausted her courage and finds herself without any escape from her peril – gripped the old soul and made her go stiff. He body needed to stretch out and no longer weigh on her weakened muscles; resting her head on the back of her chair and relaxing her limbs, the sick woman felt some relief. But that large dark bed, closed in all round by red damask curtains, but that large bed occupying by itself the whole of the room, where five years ago her husband had died, that bed increased her terror. Now she would never enter it again; she would feel as if she were entombing herself for ever, suffocating. She had, on the contrary, preserved throughout her perturbation a craving for plenty of air and light; she loathed isolation, through the illusion that contact with and the sight of strong, young and happy things would slowly renew her.

So when Gustavo, her younger son, gently persuaded her, she asked them to put a little bed for her in the room at the corner of the house, above the big penthouse with the orange trees, facing south-west, where the sky could be seen, where there were two large windows open to let the sunlight in.

As soon as she had settled down, as soon as she had the presentiment that she would never perhaps get up again, her terror was succeeded by a remarkable calm. She was waiting now; and there is nothing sadder than that long wait, than that slow wasting away of a human creature, than that certainty of being consecrated to death.

Her new room had bare walls, and the appearance of somewhere that had not been lived in for a long time. Through the panes of one of the two windows one could see right across the plain, the dark line of the hills, and behind the hills, on the bright sky, the outline of Montecorno, that smooth figure of a supine goddess which, beneath a fall of snow, looks like an immense marble statue which has been knocked down by the side of the Abruzzi region, the patroness of the old homeland, whom the mariners greet from the coast with an effusion of love, as once the sailors of Piraeus greeted Athena's spear. Beneath the other window a row of orange trees was lit up under the bright sunlight.

And the days passed. Valerio was far away, and he would not return for two, or even three months perhaps. Silence spread out through the whole house from the sick woman's bed; it was that suffocation or attenuation of all noises, of all voices which is enforced around sick people in order not to disturb their rest. The doctor, a little man whose face was clean-shaven, almost polished, came every evening, a little before sunset, at the same hour. Shadows were starting to enter the room, broken at times by one last ray which came in from the middle window and skimmed the bed; a servant brought in the light under a large green shade. When the doctor had gone, Gustavo and Francesca stayed in the room, sitting by the bed, silently, under that steady light, listening to the faint voices coming from the distant countryside. Eva's head was nodding in sleep, her hair flowing over her mother's knees, her breath issuing from beneath her hair, without her mouth being visible. Her hair was a soft, palpitating mass.

'Listen to it,' Francesca said once to her brother-in-law, caressing the hair with the satisfaction that happy mothers have.

Gustavo ran his fingers lightly through it, drawing near by bending his body without rising from his seat, and, as he did so, their hands met fleetingly. However, the two young people withdrew their hands from that contact instinctively. They looked at each other afterwards, with the curious wonder of those who have all at once discovered for an instant something that was until then unexpected, hidden: previously, neither of them had thought that such a spark would have been struck by the touch of their skin. And together they looked at the old woman: Donna Clara was sleeping; she had her eyes closed, so she must be asleep. For a moment they stayed listening to that rather hoarse breathing which weighed on the silence.

'Oh, Mamma!' murmured Eva's voice, as from amid her hair her face poked out, wrinkled in the annoying confusion of having just woken up.

2

Then in those two different natures a strange feeling was born, a mixture of regret and fear, in the depths of which a vague, tumultuous desire began to take shape: as when, during sleep, from places of rest within, where they slumber, the ghosts of past sensations and fragments of forgotten fancies start to come confusedly into sight; as when, at the collision of a body with calm, clear water, the accumulated detritus of time rises up. Then certain tiny previous events came back to mind in a new light, took on a significance which formerly they had not had, an appearance which formerly they had not had.

Francesca had come to that house little more than a month ago, to stay there during her husband's absence: the seven years of her marriage had been passed almost entirely in Naples with Valerio. Francesco remembered that, on the day of her arrival, after she had embraced Donna Clara, she had raised her face to Gustavo, and Gustavo, as he kissed her, had flushed in his hermit-like boorishness. One morning, while she and Gustavo were sitting in the orangery and Gustavo was reading to her out of a newspaper the account of a love affair, she had said, laughing and showing the pink of her upper gums:

'We were alone and we had no misgivings.'[24]

So she had spoken, with that beautiful heedless nonchalance of hers; and her laughter gave a subtle expression to her face, to that pure oval like those in Indian miniatures, the eyes drawn rising at an angle to the temples, and the eyebrows, arching too much perhaps and separating themselves from the eyelids, giving to the physiognomy a strange air of childishness.

Another morning Eva, taken with one of her usual desires to romp, had wanted Gustavo to carry her along the avenue on his shoulders, running under the boughs which were starting to bud once more; then, as soon as she saw her mother appear in the distance, a new whim took her fancy; she wanted her mother to interlace her fingers with Gustavo's, and on that interlacement she sat, throwing her little arms round both their necks, shrieking loudly in their ears.

All these events and other insignificant ones now came back to mind, in a modified form, very vividly. At night Francesca, after her first agitation and her first resistance to the temptations of unhealthy imaginings, allured by that subtle scent of guilt which rose from the depths of it all to provoke her sensibility as a young woman, gradually let herself go down the slippery slope. And as she yielded to sleep's embrace, hesitating at that point when the activity of the conscience is weakened by the relaxation of the nerves and no longer has the power to moderate the expansiveness of fancy, she went down that slope to the end, faint with desire for the sweet sin of Guido's daughter[25]. Nor would that be the first time that Francesca had sinned. She had come to matrimony at that stage which most women inevitably reach, for the very happy reasons which Dr Rondibilis expounds to the good Panurge.[26] She had already gone rapidly through two or three love affairs, emanating nothing but the radiance of youth, and going on afterwards unscathed. Hers was one of those womanly natures in which the spirit's fickleness, and the ease with which sudden sensations occur, keep passion at a distance; one of those natures resistant to suffering through the same innate quality superior metals have of resisting the corruption of oxidisation. She brought to love a sensuality that was subtle and apparently almost ingenuously curious; in fact this curiosity was precisely the unusual side of her outlook on love. When men, those two or three of them, had on their knees poured out to her all the vulgar eloquence of their hearts, she looked at them attentively with her beautiful olive eyes, not without a slightly ironic air, as though she were listening to discover whether for once they would by chance have a new accent, a new expression. Then she smiled, yielding, or rather conceding herself with a kind of lordly condescension. So great outbursts and great ardour outraged her: she did not wish for excitement, she did not understand the brutality that there can be in pleasure. She preferred a merry comedy, in good taste, crackling with humour, well executed, to serious drama badly acted. This was the result of a happy disposition, and also of an unusual artistic education, because the healthy enjoyment of art gradually generates in healthy women a kind of amiable scepticism and joyful fickleness which preserves them from passion.

Gustavo, on the contrary, little more than twenty years old, had lived these last years almost entirely in the country, with Donna Clara, in obscurity, loving lively horses and the big white greyhound inherited from his father. His spirit was uncultured, wavering, crossed at times by vague fits of melancholy, shaken by sudden agitations. That was because in him the bitter exuberance of puberty, having been suffocated, returned sometimes with the same determination to live as have the roots of couch grass settled in the earth. So when the spark flew, all those latent forces erupted with fresh violence. And in the night it was an enormous anguish, under whose weight the young man remained prostrate, an anguish where remorse was already sharpening its point, where already a dark presentiment of disaster was making itself felt, where all kinds of spectres rose up and became enormous and pressed upon him without pause. He felt he was suffocating; he heard the whole room filling with the beating of his heart, and heard words coming through those heartbeats, his mother's words. His mother was perhaps calling him from the other room? She had perhaps heard him suffering?

He raised himself on his elbow, pricking up his ears in the dark, without being able to distinguish any sound through that deafening noise. Feeling uncertain, he lit the lamp; he went through the door, he approached the sick woman's bed. She turned her dazzled eyes away from the light.

'What do you want, Gustavo?'

'Didn't you call me?'

'No, my boy.'

'I thought, Mamma, I heard…'

'Go and sleep. God bless you, my son.'

3

The following morning Gustavo was returning slowly down the avenue, together with Famulus, the large, snow-white dog which followed him with that dance-like swaying which is so gentle and elegant in greyhounds. It was one of those virginal mornings of early spring, when the countryside has something like a convalescent's indolence upon wakening. A milky haze, a limpid glimmer, was roving across the green, under the trees; and over everything the sun shed a reddish-white radiance, an indistinct tremulousness. The old earth of the Abruzzi was now being aroused.

In the distance, at the end of the avenue, against the dark green of the orange trees, Gustavo noticed a white speck, like those which statues make in gardens. But, while he was straining his eyes, the dog sped off from his side, as if it had scented its prey, with one of those stupendous dashes, like an antelope in flight.

'Famulus, here! Famulus!'

It was Francesca's voice, among the trees. She stood waiting for the greyhound to reach her, snapping her fingers, sending that ringing call into the air. When Gustavo came up with her, she was already bending over the dog, squeezing its long muzzle between her caressing hands: she was very beautiful – in her richly pleated morning dress, inside

75

which the suppleness of her living body could be imagined, with the hair on the nape of her neck gathered up and held in a knot on the top of her head as in certain eighteenth-century portraits – bent like that over the animal which lay on its back and waved its thin, nervous paws at her, showing its slender, flesh-coloured stomach.

'Good morning, Signora.'

'Oh, Gustavo, good morning!' she answered, raising herself vivaciously, her face slightly flushed from having bent down. And while she offered him her hand, she looked at him curiously with half-closed eyes, for she had risen from her bed beautifully serene. Then altering her voice in fun, she added:

'Where have you come from, O Signore?'

Gustavo understood and smiled: through weak, boyish hesitation he had not called her by name in his greeting; now he was sorry, had much to say, and wanted to speak in a self-assured manner.

'A long way, Francesca. I went out at daybreak, taking Famulus with me. The air was bracing. We've gone through the fields, through the pinewood… The pinewood is all blooming with violets; the scent of the resin is mingled with the scent of the flowers… If you'd smelt it! We'll go there on horseback, one day, when you want to… We went by the farm at the foot of the hills; the meadow is soaked in heavy dew. The rabbits were running away on all sides. Famulus grabbed one by the neck; I made him let it go. We went right round, and then came to the avenue. Famulus saw you a long way off, and he ran to you to lick your hands. You're giving too many pieces of sugar to this old glutton: you'll spoil him, Francesca…'

He went on speaking, because Francesca was listening to him. Then Eva appeared, looking scared, and shouted:

'Come quickly, Mamma! Grandma is feeling ill.'

They ran together. They found Donna Clara in bed, suffering one of those nervous attacks of coldness which made her tremble all over, shaking her poor bones. She could not speak; an almost livid pallor was on her face, her chin was quivering rapidly and her eyes looked lost in their sockets beneath their half-closed lids. She could do nothing to help herself; she had to wait for the moment to pass. Gustavo placed his warm hand on her frozen forehead, leaning, with an expression of fear and tenderness, towards that poor livid face, breathing warm air onto her face, calling her softly, at times with his mouth against her ear. She must have heard, because the irises reappeared in her yellowish eyeballs, and on her lips a vain attempt at a smile was struggling against the convulsive shaking. The sun was not yet coming into the room; a blaze of gold was breaking on the closed panes. Gradually the sick woman's shuddering ceased; two or three times she opened her mouth to take in air, at intervals, weakly. As the heat gradually penetrated her, the pallor of her face became milder. She turned her eyes to those who stood around; now she could smile, lowering her eyelids, without speaking. An immense tiredness pervaded all her being; and in that prostration she still preserved the horror which had shaken her; meanwhile, in front of the growing happiness of the spring morning, a bitter regret, the regret for something irremediable, was sobbing in her. It was all over; she was old, and so she had to die. And the weariness went on pervading her: a bewilderment of the senses, a heavy warmth possessed her from head to foot.

'She's falling asleep,' murmured Francesca.

'No, she's fainting,' said Gustavo. He was pale, for he had felt the life-beat weakening in his mother's pulse.

'Run, Gustavo: up in my room, by the bed, there is a crystal phial. Bring it here.'

He went, ran up the stairs, went into the room. Despite his filial agitation, a strong impression of scent and freshness struck him in the face and made him start; an impression of red light, like a great cloud of pink dust, where the warm exhalations of the bath were swimming, where the natural scent of female skin, that disturbing perfume, was still alive. He searched for the phial by the bed, he searched for it without looking: on the bed the rumpled bedclothes revealed the whiteness of the sheet where there still remained the impression of the body which had lain there. Francesca's scent rose from it, that scent which she customarily had.

As he searched he placed his hand on something soft: it was perhaps a folded blouse, who knows, something which she must already have worn. The strong scent remained on his hands. He found the phial, went out, and ran down again.

4

…Just past midday. The previous evening they had at long last decided to ride to the pinewood: and that afternoon, as March was dying, was alluring.

They went along the great avenue. They rode side by side at a hunting trot, silently at first. Gustavo compelled his bay to fall a little behind, so that he could look at the slender, upright figure of Francesca who, encased in her black riding-habit, with her mass of chestnut hair gathered up beneath her elegant felt hat, kept her sorrel at that light trot with the firm pressure of her glove. She was concentrating on the delight of feeling the wind in her face, of feeling her soul striking with a nervous foot on the elastic, sonorous ground. When one of her curls got in her eyes, she threw it back from her temples with a lively motion of her head. On one occasion she hit an obstructing hedge with her crop, bending towards that side; a flock of birds rose noisily into the blue, into the blue which was laughing between the clouds with that diffused sweetness there is after rain on the astonished countryside. In the country one could feel then the pacific influence of the snowy *Goddess*, of that figure which made the most splendid outline in the land around. Farm-workers were scattered through the sown fields.

'To the left, Francesca,' warned Gustavo, pressing forward.

They came across two pairs of yoked oxen, with red tassels, perhaps just taken from the cart, led by a kind of old satyr holding the ropes in his hand.

The sorrel broke out of the trot, changing its motion into a gentle gallop, without going ahead. Francesca held the reins short, bending forward, in a bold attitude, to look at the animal's hooves in their graceful playfulness. Gustavo, in his admiration, said that the sorrel could have galloped within the circumference of a golden napoleon. Then Francesca was seized with an adventurous desire to race: her pink nostrils dilated as she smelt the wind.

'Hip! Hip! Hip! Hurrah!'

The horses moved impulsively as one, their animation growing: those beautiful young beasts had also scented the spring.

'Hip!'

The horsewoman was growing excited: the fresh, almost cold wind put some red on her cheeks, put a curve on her lips between which her teeth appeared and a little of the upper gums. She had one of those times of happy forgetfulness which healthy people enjoy, when they are delighted by the exercise of strength and agility and affected by lively sensations. And as expansive good-heartedness is naturally born out of joy, she now felt herself attracted to Gustavo, who was galloping by her side, she now felt that effusion of well-being was joining her to him.

'Hip! Hip!'

They did not look at each other, but they felt that deep enchantment which comes from looking into someone else's eyes. The road was bending sharply; a little bridge over a canal resounded at their passage; the pinewood was blackening in the distance, setting against the sky the same rising waves which the backs of a mass of beasts, particularly sheep, form when they are on the road.

'The pinewood!' Gustavo was the first to cry, pointing with his crop in that direction. The resinous aroma was borne on the wind. And, turning a little towards his companion, the horseman said:

'Breathe it in, Francesca. This scent does you good.'

He said these simple words in an indescribable tone of voice, as he would have spoken the vehement beginning of a love lyric. The festival of his youth burst out luminously; he did not repress it, he did not wish to repress it. No kind of happiness is sweeter than being at the loved one's side, on horseback, riding through the birth of spring to a loving destination. Those upsurgings of barbaric freedom, which men have in their blood, made him now forget his brother. His brother's wife was beautiful and he was winning her.

'Hip! Hip!'

The pinewood was close; the sun penetrated the wood, leaving gleaming areas among the tall trees, and through the brightness flights of fabulous porticoes fled away into the distance. They entered at a walk, slackening the reins while the horses panted noisily, shaking their heads or bringing their nostrils close to the riders as though to speak to them in secret. In front of them flights of frightened birds rose into the air. Above their heads the sky occasionally opened up and, amid the green, its azure was changed into a gentle violet.

So they explored the wood. Through the labyrinth, between trunk and trunk, the horses could not walk together. Francesca went on ahead, a little tired from the race, caressing with her open hand the sorrel's steaming neck. Gustavo came behind, in silence. But from the bushes a sharp perfume, from flowers that could not be seen, rose up: a perfume that disturbed them and made them feel desire. They were in one of those glades, for the most part circular, where the charm of the wood could be felt in a livelier and more penetrating way.

'Ah, Gustavo, look at that flower!' exclaimed Francesca, pointing. 'If you hold my crop for me, I shall gather it myself.'

And, having given him the crop, she leant from the saddle with a supple movement; meanwhile the sorrel was striking the ground with one bent leg. It is something which usually happens in any riding-expedition involving two people, in novels and in real life.

It was a small red flower, with a subtle fragrance.

'Smell it, Gustavo,' she said, and brought it to his nostrils.

A temptation: Gustavo grazed her fingers with his hot mouth, trembling. She said nothing, but her face changed a little; and she urged her horse forward.

'Listen, Francesca, a moment!' the young man cried out to her from behind, and urged his horse too. It was almost a pursuit through the dangerously dense trees, a sonorous trampling on dried pine cones among the bushes. One of her arms had struck against a trunk, with a dry sound.

'Stop, stop! You'll do yourself harm.'

She had come to the thick of the wood, where the horses refused to go further. The tall pines rose, upright and inflexible, in the inmost recesses of the wood. All around, in the green light, nothing but trees, trees!

'Stop!'

And they found themselves face to face, pale and hesitating; and the horses were straining at the bit and pawing the ground.

'You've knocked your arm. Do you feel ill?' asked Gustavo in a hoarse, tender voice. He compelled his horse to draw near, took hold of Francesca's arm lightly, unbuttoned her sleeve at the wrist. Francesca let him do it, as she looked on. The sleeve of her riding habit was so tight! Between her glove and the black cloth her wrist was disclosed, round and snowy, a wrist lined with veins like the forehead of a child. Gustavo, holding her wrist between his fingers, tried with his other hand to pull the sleeve up. The horse shook the reins which had been left free on its neck.

'See!'

On her arm, near the elbow, there was a red mark which was beginning to turn blue, a nasty little wound on the whiteness of the skin which was soft with down. Gustavo wanted to kiss her. But then Francesca rapidly – doing it very beautifully – rapidly yielded her mouth to Lanciotto's brother, while the vexed horses pawed the ground.

They turned back on their tracks to leave the wood. The sunset raised a greater abundance of incense from the thickets where the sun's rays were dying amid a last vision of fabulous porticoes. And then, on the wet meadow, the white and grey rabbits fled before the trotting horses, with their tails erect, and disappeared in the midst of the new grass.

5

When, on their return, they entered Donna Clara's room, that strange odour which there is in the air breathed by sick people, that odour struck their nostrils displeasingly; because they still had the lively sensation of the sylvan emanations and of the wind blowing on the meadowland.

Donna Clara remained an instant without opening her eyes, supine, in one of those fitful spells of drowsiness which came over her towards evening. She was there: she wore a bewildered expression, as of someone who had lost consciousness. A white band covered her forehead, the bedcovers reached to her chin; out of all that heartbreaking whiteness came the outline of her wasted nose, an almost diaphanous outline; and the general shape of her body was lost beneath the folds of the bedcovers.

Francesca and Gustavo remained standing, opposite each other, at either side of the bed, without raising their eyes, because that suffering old woman's body divided them, put them at a distance from each other. They felt themselves tempted, even in the presence of that sadness, by impatience, the impatience of someone who, though urged by desire, has to repress it and suffer an annoying delay. There was now a force urging them together. But Gustavo, as the son, realised faintly that their impatience was cruel; and to escape from that thought he gave himself those internal reproofs and exhortations men do give themselves, in the theatre of their conscience, in the presence of a guilty feeling. Was that poor sick woman then no longer his mother? Did he then no longer feel the old fondness for her? After having been such a long time away from her, did it then seem to him hard to stay in her room and look at her for a little while? And why? Had he become wicked all of a sudden, and insensible? He asked himself these questions, but without much attention, as though he were acting a noble part to dodge the accusation. The thoughts and the fancies of the recent afternoon of love distracted him, obsessed him.

Eventually Donna Clara opened her eyes, with an effort. She said nothing, she replied to questions only with a slight lowering of her eyelids and a fleeting smile. The sight of the two of them had given her no comfort; on the contrary, a streak of bitterness ran through her soul, because she had been abandoned by them for too long. That day she had heard Francesca laughing down in the avenue, Gustavo talking, and then the trampling of the horses disappearing into the distance. She was left alone; Eva had run in a little while later.

'Listen, Eva, be a good girl and open that window.'

The toddler had assumed a nurse's serious air. She could not manage to open the window, even though she stood on tiptoe.

'Call Susanna. You can't do it.'

'Oh, Grandma, what are you saying?'

She had dragged a chair into the bay of the window, in order to climb on it and open the window. She opened it. The grandmother looked at her and smiled: enveloped in the bright dust which rose from the floor, with her little arms bare, the toddler had the agility and grace of a goat which tries to reach the top of a hedge.

Warm breaths of air had come in through the half-opened window;

all the fields could be glimpsed, under the protection of the sun.

'Like this, Grandma?'

'Yes. You're a good girl, Eva. Come here.'

The old woman had felt herself growing tender; she felt the need to press that sweet mass of hair to her breast, to rest her cheek there a moment. And so she took refuge in the adoration of that childish head.

Then Eva too had gone away, down into the garden, to run on the grass. The air was blowing too strongly through the window; the wind was getting up; the curtains were fluttering and swelling out; the harsh, clear light came in like rising waters. Then the sick woman had started to shudder, as once more she was seized by that nervous coldness that she found so painful. She had hardly had the strength to ring the bell to call someone. Susanna had come, that fat and noisy woman, to press her rough hand to her forehead and invoke the Virgins in heaven...

Were Francesca and Gustavo returning from their walk then? So late? Had they never given a thought to her?

Francesca wanted to break the silence, which was weighing on her.

'Do you know, Mamma? We've been to the pinewood.'

'Ah.'

'It was later than we realised.'

'Ah.'

'I've brought you this flower.'

At these last words Gustavo pulled himself together: that go-between, the flower, still had a subtle fragrance which reached as far as him; and the scent reawakened the ghost of the fleeting kiss and the distant glade.

Donna Clara stretched her thin, trembling hand out of the covers to take the flower.

6

At that moment the moon rose slowly through the trees, chaste and silvery, according to custom; and it shone on the window-panes and overcame the weak light shed through the green shade of the lamp indoors.

Donna Clara had closed her eyes again. Some minutes later she said in a weak voice to the two of them, who had remained standing there in silence:

'You must be tired... Send Susanna to me... Go to supper.'

They left the room; it was almost as if they felt the relief of children released from punishment, they smiled into each other's eyes.

'Oh Mamma, oranges!' cried Eva, running to Francesca, embracing her knees in an impulse of joy, with an orange clasped in each hand. She clambered up her, so it seemed, to her hips, with the agility of a squirrel, and clasped her neck, breathing on her face a breath that smelt of the fruit she had sucked.

'Would you like these oranges?'

They went into the red dining-room; they sat down to a supper which Eva filled with her noise, with the tiny charms of a greedy child. Unconsciously, she became an accomplice.

'Oh Mamma, peel the orange for me.'

Her mother thrust her thin, pink nails into the fragrant peel to open it up: her fingers got wet with the juice which was pressed out, and a light golden colour remained on them. Eva looked on with the voracity of a famished rodent. When the fruit was bare, she sacrificed one segment to her mother and Gustavo.

'This half for one,' she said gravely. 'Bite it, Mamma.'

Francesca broke the half segment between her teeth, smiling.

'Now your turn.'

Gustavo took the other half between his lips; it was a delicious sensation.

In the room there was that warmth which comes from the steam of hot dishes, that warmth that instils into the blood a laziness, a slug-gish bliss, after a meal. Light came down peacefully from the hanging porcelain globe.

Gustavo got up, and went to open the window.

'What a marvellous moon!' he exclaimed, because in him, who had eaten hardly anything, the sentimentality of a new lover was stimulated by that brightness.

Francesca made a gesture of annoyance: the cold air coming in was disturbing the pleasant heat into which she had settled, and it disturbed that abandonment, crowded with rambling fantasies and indeterminate desires, in which she was about to delude herself.

'For heaven's sake, close it, Gustavo!'

'Come and look for a moment.'

She got up from her chair with an effort; as she came up she shivered, and gathered herself together, hiding her hands in the broad sleeves of her dress; instinctively, she drew near to Gustavo.

In front of them, in the immensity of the night, fell the rays of the moon, the peace of the moon, where everything that was submerged in it presented the indistinct vision of submarine depths with their great animal flora full of a fearful swarming. The region's mountains, covered in snow, were coming nearer, almost leaning over the plain: at one glance it was possible to descend into all the hollows of shadow, climb all the luminous heights. They looked like the vertebrae of a land whose sun had been extinct for centuries; they gave the impression of a lunar landscape seen through a telescope.

They looked, in silence. For a moment they were dominated by that natural scene. They stood close to each other, touching with their elbows, touching with their knees.

Behind them Eva was playing on the table, shredding the orange peel which was left on the plates, murmuring empty words, waiting for sleep to take her in its arms.

Gustavo gently slid his fingers into Francesca's sleeves, and held her bare hand under the covering material.

'Stop, Gustavo, stop!' she said, turning round, worrying about Eva; and as she turned she breathed on his neck.

He did not understand; he felt, beneath his skin which was cold in the night air, all the blood in his heart rise into his face in a blaze.

He had taken both her hands, and bent to cover them with kisses.

'No, not here, Gustavo…'

He did not understand. Francesca freed one hand from his grasp; to push him away she sank one hand into his hair, and raised his head. Then she distanced herself, approached the table; she was trembling all over.

'How cold it is!' she said. 'Shut the window.'

Gustavo put his forehead out into the fresh air and remained for an instant with his breast leaning towards the night. In this way he hoped to calm the tumult, the heat. Then he closed the window; he turned; he was pale, with his mouth twitching somewhat.

Francesca had taken refuge by Eva.

The toddler's head was nodding over the table, over the snow-white tablecloth, because she was falling asleep; she was pink, all pink, with a vague smile all over her face; her closed eyelids were so diaphanous that they seemed to let her glance come through; she was breathing very gently.

'Sleep,' whispered her mother. And she made a sign to Gustavo to walk quietly.

'I'll carry her up to the room,' said Gustavo quietly.

She scented danger in those words, and smiled with a lightly ironic movement of her lower lip. But Gustavo had drawn near; he took the little motionless body of Eva tenderly in his arms. In this way they ascended the stairs: Francesca in front, Gustavo behind. The toddler's head hung down on one side, revealing her soft throat, letting her hair pour down.

In the room a lamp was burning under a shade, giving an almost lunar light. From the clothes, from the linen, from every corner perfumes were exhaled and hovered in the air.

'Put her down on the bed, there.'

Gustavo laid the toddler down. His arms were already trembling: he smelt the perfume which had on one occasion made him jump. Francesca was bending over her daughter, watching her sleep, waiting for Gustavo to speak. He did not speak; he took her suddenly by the arm, and put his mouth to the nape of her neck where two or three little curls were white with powder. He had in his eyes a dark glitter and in his face a dark passion which Francesca recognised. But Francesca did not want this: the violence of it displeased her.

'No, no, Gustavo. Go,' she said in a serious voice, rearranging the hair on her nape. 'Be sensible.'

Then in him all the repressed wave of passion erupted. He loved her! He felt he was going mad. If she would only let him stay there one hour, kneeling on the carpet, in that room, in that perfume! He was asking for nothing more: if she were kind!

'No, go. Eva will wake up.'

He went on urging her. Eva was in her first sleep: she could not wake up. He would stay there without moving. If she would let him stay; a little longer, a little longer!

He had drawn near to her again, he was holding her wrists, he was pleading with his look; he wanted to conquer her slowly. Francesca felt that she would yield because she sensed a sweetness and a vague weariness starting to overcome her. Two or three times she cast her eyes around, disquieted, because Gustavo had seized her by her waist and was drawing her to him. She rebelled for one last time against the languor.

'But you do know, Gustavo, what we are doing?'

Gustavo clasped her, searching for her mouth. He loved her! He loved her!

7

From then on they let themselves be entangled and drawn along, Francesca through her compliance and unthinking frivolity, Gustavo through his blind greed for love. And since love overpowers and abases every other human feeling, they now abandoned the sick woman.

It was a sad business, which they accomplished quite naturally. The pleasant time of year enticed them out of doors, the open air delighted them, the overflowing vitality of growing things entered into them from all sides. At home, they were annoyed and irritated by the effort required to repress every word, to suppress every noise. They went out, and were absent for long periods, absorbed in each other; they preferred remote places – refuges sheltered by trees, paths straying through the estate. Gustavo brought to their meeting-places the enthusiasm of his passion, all the vehemence of his almost virginal nature; Francesca contributed the attractive fickleness of her looks, the faint cruelty of her calmness, her imperious refinement of sensation. They fled instinctively from everything, from all circumstances which might lead them to be conscious of themselves. As they went out, nearly always one of them said, as though in self-justification:

'It seems better, doesn't it? No one ever complains.'

And they went.

But Donna Clara, in that bare room, in the presence of that splendour which poured down onto the floor through the half-closed blinds, felt a gloomy anguish which was killing her; she felt that the end was near. She had not guessed at first: she remained supine in her bed, for long hours, in the grip of her illness, with her troubled eyes already sightless, with her extremities icy cold, as if she had already begun to die in an agony that would be long and without a tremor. At times her skinny hands made those restless, uncertain, searching motions, that futile clenching of fists trying to take hold of something. Then she wanted to drink, she wanted the cup to relieve the dryness of her jaws. Susanna came to the door every now and then; she approached, she put the cup to the sick woman's mouth, holding her head up with one hand.

'Where are... they?'

'Eh, madam, who knows?'

Donna Clara started: Susanna had spoken with a treacherous note in her voice. Where were they going? What were they doing all that time out of doors? Ah, was that what it was for? Suddenly she saw the light; and, together with the suspicion which was quickly growing, a violent anger suddenly took hold of her. Ah, was that what it was for? Oh, vile creatures! Oh, vile creatures! Oh, vile creatures!

Then Eva came in, stepping lightly, carrying a bunch of flowers in her arms which were bare to the elbows. She came up to the bed, smiling; she was so beautiful. But when she felt her head taken between the old woman's damp, burning hands, and felt on her hair, on her neck, on her cheeks so many hot drops, so many tears fall, and amongst the tears she felt that dry mouth with its breath heavy with illness moving towards her forehead, and heard her father's name brokenly through those piercing sobs, she was aghast and tried to free herself, to catch hold of the hand that was holding her, and look into the old woman's face; she choked out:

'What's wrong? What's wrong?...'

Ad Altare Dei

1

It is a joy to remember. When the bells began to ring and the waves of sound began to spread out all over the blessed earth, we stopped in our tracks.

'It's the Purification,' said Giacinta.

Ave Maria!

I remember: she was all white, in an almost nun-like dress. Its folds were abundant on her breast, they clasped her tightly at the waist, then they fell down again freely to her feet. On the skin of her neck, her nape, her temples spread a pleasing tint of gold, something indefinably golden and transparent, beneath the scarcely visible down. Against the pallor of her cheeks the pearls hanging from her pink, shell-like ears trickled with a vague splendour that was at times slightly opaque. Part of her nape was bare, and on it flourished a wonderful cloud of hair: the rest of her neck was covered by the high white veil of a scarf, under the twisting pearls: the rest of her hair was fastened in a big tawny knot, and spread out on both sides under a dusting of powder which made it look ashen.

I remember everything.

She said, '*Ave Maria!*' innocently. Then she smiled at me with that wide mouth of hers. And we stayed a moment listening to the bells sounding out at that great festival on a February morning.

We were in the vicinity of Fontanella. On those heights the last white vapour was rising from the ground and melting into the air; and as the heights descended to the plain, the vapour was succeeded by the bright sparkle of recent frost. All the ground seemed crystallised, and on that changeable background of splendours the bare trees rose up like a cold efflorescence of stone. On one side a large group of grey fig trees made monstrous shapes with their branches. I still remember that certain other trees with numerous slender branches, elms perhaps, perhaps poplars, gave me the childish impression of gigantic millipedes standing on end.

Giacinta was praying: I saw her lips moving as she uttered the syllables softly. I looked at her. She was not truly beautiful, with a classical beauty; when she smiled her mouth widened and rose on both sides to the lobes of her ears, but her teeth had a gemlike brightness; her eyes had small irises and their great globes were softened by that slight tint of indigo which is common in babies. I liked her like this. She had already disturbed my virginal childhood with something like a germ of love. She was more than sixteen, a woman.

And after a moment she said: 'Let's go to the church.'

We walked side by side, hardly disturbing the silence with a single word. On one side extended the dead vines with their red shoots, awaiting the pruning-hook, because they had a foreboding of spring; on the other side stretched the furrows of grain in its green and delicate infancy. When we turned into the road for Chieti, a flock of sheep looked at us as we went by: the gentle black and white animals stood with their heads held up, their ears rosy against the light, on the short grass in the morning idyll; and two or three sucklings were seeking out the dugs between their mothers' legs.

Giacinta smiled almost tenderly, turning away; she was devout.

2

The church was at the end of an avenue sheltered by oaks which had the gravity of patriarchs and were as old as gods. Outside the avenue, the peeling of the plaster disclosed the reddish bricks, and at the sides half-moon windows were open. On the blunt spire of the façade a cross of iron held out its arms. The architecture of the church was simple and crude, like those outlines which boys draw on the margins of books they hate. Around, on the square, appeared the houses of the peasants, tall heaps of dry straw. I still preserve an impression of colour: the perforated blocks of vermilion terracotta on certain very tall, contorted tree trunks against that sky of an almost spiritual blue. And I can still see the hollow face of that sick woman who stretched out her hand to us for alms by the door. A face of an indefinable hue, where all that remained alive were the two sad, glaucous eyes of a solitary toad in the shade of a black kerchief with little yellow flowers tied under the chin. A hand reminiscent of the hairy webbed foot of a duck.

Giacinta and I went into the church with the crowd. The deferential peasants let us pass through the strong smell of the olive oil gleaming on their hair. We came to the middle; where it was starting to slope down towards the altar, was the harvest of kneeling Christians, a great varied harvest of heads covered in silk kerchiefs – yellow, red, black, spotted, striped, flowered. The altar rose up, flaming with votive candles whose rays were reflected on the zinc holders placed beneath them, on the fake gold plating of the ciborium, on the artificial flowers of silver thread and wool. By the altar, on an eminence, the Virgin stood over the crowding faithful; the Queen of all Virgins, all beautiful in her dress of azure satin with golden embroidery, all glorious with her diadem of white metal adorned with great stones, all lit up by the adoration of those sinful souls who were begging for pardon.

Giacinta and I remained standing, held against each other by the pressure of the crowd, silent, looking on. In the air, warm already with so many human breaths, amid the exhalations of the crowd hovered the sharp odour of jonquils, of violets, and rosemary. A dim light came down from the half-moon windows covered with red curtains. Nothing could be heard but the roaring of the bellows in the organ and, at times, when someone opened the door to come in, the hoarse, plaintive voice of the sick beggar-woman.

'*Introibo ad altare Dei. Ad Deum qui laetificat juventutem meam...*'[27] the priest began at the foot of the altar.

Giacinta was motionless, listening. She alone, in the middle of all that confusion of colours, in half-light; she alone was erect and slender, emerging like a tall water-flower leaning towards the light. And she believed; she was devout. Near to us, I recall, rose a kind of tabernacle of dark wood, enclosed by three glass windows, which held the statue of San Rocco in painted plaster. We were under the saint's protection. A stray dog, crouching at the pedestal, lifted its muzzle towards its protector; and the black-bearded martyr, pointing with his left hand to a purple wound on his bare knee, supporting himself with his pilgrim's staff in his right hand, was staring into a void with two eyes of white, drilled glass. Above the tabernacle hung two matching feet and one arm, roughly shaped in wax, reddish, like real mutilated human limbs, as votive offerings.

'*Confitebor tibi in cithara, Deus, Deus meus!*'[28] continued the priest, in his hollow voice, at the foot of the altar. The organ up aloft created deep, soft harmonies, changing its tone at every moment. This instrument's shining pipes were above the top of the baldachin; and there, behind, in the choir, from a rent in a curtain the sun suddenly appeared and stretched out through the air a band of gold all swarming with motes. One part of Christ crucified was darkly outlined on that glorious stripe.

'*Gloria Patri, et Filio, et Spiritui Sancto…*'[29]

The whole crowd bowed down in concentration, and the organ's great voice, in response, dominated the hoarse chant of the priest. The shade had increased in contrast with the sun in the choir; the warmth was growing, fed by the breath of those who were kneeling, a heavy warmth which induced drowsiness, which exhausted the spirit in the sluggish contemplation of its god.

'*Domine exaudi orationem meam.*'[30]

Giacinta and I were pressed against each other. A sort of weakening began to take hold of me, intense heat rose into my face; a strange sensation came to me from all that conglomeration of people over whom the wave of prayer was passing, in the darkness broken by the tremulous gleams from the altar. I too believed; and the sacred organ sounds and the sweet odour which emanated from Giacinta aroused confused visions from my childhood faith, infinite visions, in the middle of which, I do not know why, flourished certain vague memories of my early childhood: the memory, for example, of all those lilies with great silver calyxes which made me drowsy with their perfume one June evening in my sister's room; the memory of a cluster of nests which I brought down from the gutter with a stick, one spring morning, in order to steal the little pearly eggs from the brooding swallows.

'*Oremus te, Domine, per merita sanctorum tuorum…*'[31]

And the organ's harmony sent a long shudder over all the heads there. Giacinta was bowing. I was holding her hand. She was taller than I; I rested my head lightly on her shoulder. I do not know what she was feeling; but my sensations were pure and mild; there was a languor moving gradually through my veins, there was a sort of tenderness which conquered my soul and made me bend my knee unconsciously and bow my head.

'*Tu solus Dominus, tu solus Altissimus, Jesu Christe…*'[32]

94

There was a confused movement throughout the kneeling crowd, something whitish passed over the whole crowd. It was perhaps their hands making the sign of the cross from forehead to heart. The organ suddenly rose to the high notes, cast into the nave the great harmony of a joyful hymn which swept across all those souls like a beam of light and lifted them up to paradise.

But among the crowd could be heard the rattle of copper coins on the plate which the altar-boy brought round; then on high there was the rasping sound of the red curtains being drawn. A great light was shed from on high; below, colours emerged into the light.

'*Kyrie eleison. Christe eleison. Kyrie eleison.*'[33]

The choir's voices, unsteady, uncertain, started up; the voices of children who could not be seen. They were like jets of water rising into that air where the February sun was spreading a cloudlike virginal bliss, like an evanescence of white specks of dust. I closed my eyes, felt a long shiver of joy, pressed against Giacinta who was following the litany in a low voice; and the instinct of love, which was slowly developing in my boyish constitution, put into that mystical joy a thin vein of sensual desire. I saw, through my eyelids, a rosy gleam, a great rosy wood in flower, through the living tissue of my eyelids.

'*Sancta Maria, ora pro nobis!*'[34]

The voices became firm and clear; the organ's cadences continued in a minor tone. The crowd showed at first an indistinct waving of heads; then, little by little, drawn along by the canticle, stupefied by the heat and the odour of mingled incense and flowers, little by little, leaned forward, leaned towards the Virgin, with one of those blind impulses which superstition promotes in simple souls. The Virgin was resplendent in the greater light; her face was white and impassive, her eyes motionless and unseeing, and in those crystal globes there was the intense attraction which is found only in the eyes of shapeless idols and dead fish.

'*Virgo prudentissima. Virgo veneranda. Virgo predicanda...*'[35]

Then all the voices burst out; there was a great canticle of all the voices, a great lifting up of praise into the air, on high, towards the nave crowned by the rays of the growing sunlight and the smoke of the thurible, on high, on high.

'Rosa mystica. Turris Davidica. Turris eburnea...'[36]

On high! An infinitely tender love invaded the kneeling crowd, an ardent and sweet breath passed over all their heads and prostrated them in prayer on the floor.

'Consolatrix afflictorum, ora pro nobis!'[37]

Giacinta was singing too, bending down, with a spiritual flush on her face, with her eyes bright, shaking like a sonorous instrument. I had not bent my knees, there was no space around me; but I was filled with a sort of foolish bewilderment, because I alone was standing above all the others around; and those human creatures so prostrate and imploring so blindly, that living mass of matter from which burst out such a high hymn of almost unconscious passion, and that sun which was filling the nave and here and there falling onto people's backs, and those vapours now nauseating and now celestial, and above everything that motionless and unbending Madonna, those motionless and unbending saints looking into a void, presented me with a fearful spectacle, unsettled my little uneducated soul.

And the hymn grew louder, the litanies went up; it seemed as if, in the long shudder, the organ-pipes would burst.

'Regina virginum, Regina sanctorum omnium, ora pro nobis!'[38]

Now the Lamb of God came into the canticle, the Lamb of God Who takes away the sins of the world. It was the final lifting up of praise.

'Ora pro nobis, Sancta Dei Genitrix!'[39]

The organ ceased; the rumble spread through the nave, and the rumble ceased. Silence fell on the church, where the believers, still prostrate, were breathing heavily. Then all their foreheads rose again, every hand was raised in the sign of the cross; a whisper ran through the crowd; through the open door a wave of fresh, purifying air came in. Broken voices came from the choir; behind the altar could be seen a confused waving of banners.

Giacinta and I were still beneath San Rocco's tabernacle. When I raised my eyes towards her, she smiled at me; but I cannot describe that smile in words: it was like the passage of something benign and luminous across a face which remained sad; it was not a movement of the mouth or eyes, no; it looked – that's it – almost like a gleam lighting up the pensive profile of a white statue; no, that's not it; I cannot find the words. Afterwards we stayed silent, waiting for the procession to start to unwind from the sacristy. In the open space in front of the door a group of men were shouting: the glory of carrying on one's shoulder the weight of Mary's image was being auctioned.

'Five *carlini*! One ducat! Two ducats!…'

The crowd waited. Almost all the women had their hands clasped on their stomachs and a dull stupidity in their eyes; the men were looking towards the door, murmuring. In the middle of them, in the path left free, an indefinite blackish mass began to move along the ground, a heap of rags, and to creep slowly towards the altar.

'Two ducats! Three ducats!'

A human head emerged from that heap, as from the shell of a tortoise the greenish head shoots out wobbling. It was the sick beggar-woman; I recognised her with a shudder of repugnance, because she no longer had the kerchief on her head: a misshapen skull appeared, gnawed all over like a disinterred skull on which there were still some locks of grey hair and some remains of a reddish scalp. And that skull advanced along the ground, driven by the body which was supported by the palms of the hands and by the knees.

'Three ducats! Three and a half ducats!'

The beggar-woman made a great many crosses with her tongue on the paving-stones, to the glory of Mary; she wanted to go to Mary's feet; she wanted to be worthy to kiss the hem of her dress. She gathered her strength, drawing herself up, thrusting with her bare toes. From both sides of the space, people watched with the indifference of those accustomed to a spectacle of horror. But a tall man, dressed in a deep blue cloak, with a great hooked nose, came up angrily; he kicked the beggar-woman, lifted her up brutally from the ground, and dragged her outside the door: 'Get away! Get away!'

'Three and a half ducats! Four ducats!'

The auction was over. The bell started to ring from behind the sacristy; then, suddenly, a great clang of bells on high made the church shake from its foundations. And the first standards processed horizontally, they came into the open air, they were lifted upright, and they fluttered: they were two purplish standards with silver lace.

Ding dong! Ding dong! Men with azure cloaks processed, with lighted candles, two by two, in a line.

Ding dong! Ding dong! A third standard processed, very tall, of dark scarlet bordered with gold, with a golden ball on the top of the pole. *Ding dong!*

The gigantic Christ processed, nailed on the cross, all splashed with bruises and blood, carried on the bulge of his stomach by a sturdy man supported by two others at his sides.

Ding dong, dong dong! The brass instruments began a triumphal march; the firecrackers were set off. Last in the procession was the Virgin of Virgins, the Morning Star, the Tower of Ivory, amid the cries of her people, and she came out into the sunlight, she came out to scatter her benediction on all the sown countryside.

'Alleluia! Alleluia!'

The crowd of enraptured women and men followed the sparkling and undulating of the mantle on high. The standards, struck by the wind, tossed and twisted themselves round their staffs. On the road the dust was raised in gusts enveloping the whole display. The red baldachin oscillated on its four gilt supports, threatening the singing priests.

Giacinta and I saw the procession go off into the distance among the patriarchal oaks, we saw the last purplish flutterings in the clear air, we saw the cross shining on the Madonna's diadem, and then we saw all those moving shapes disappear in the blazing sun which watched over the deserted countryside...

NOTES

1. 'Peace to this house.'

2. 'You will sprinkle me with hyssop, Lord, and I shall be cleansed…'

3. 'Hear us, Holy Lord…'

4. 'Have mercy…'

5. 'Behold the Lamb of God, behold Him who takes away the sins of the world…'

6. 'Let us pray…'

7. 'Lest You call to mind [our sins].'

8. 'May the Lord be kind to you, however you have transgressed. Amen.'

9. 'Lord have mercy. Christ have mercy. Lord have mercy. Our Father [who art in heaven…].'

10. St Thecla of Iconium is recorded in the Apocrypha as being an apostle of St Paul – she dedicated herself to a chaste life and twice was miraculously saved from death; St Euphemia of Chalcedon (d. AD 308) was also a virgin martyr who was burnt to death, but whose body was not completely destroyed by the fire.

11. Behold the handmaid of the Lord.

12. 'Remember! Remember, [man, that you are dust, and will return to dust].'

13. Blessed is he who comes in the name of the Lord. Hosanna in the highest!

14. 'Let us proceed in peace.'

15. 'In the name of Christ. Amen.'

16. The *Finanzieri* is an Italian army corps (similar to *Carabinieri*), founded in 1881 after the Unification of Italy.

17. Joel II.28.

18. 'Let us therefore humbly venerate so great a sacrament…'

19. In Virgil's *Eclogues* (37 BC) Galatea features as a shepherdess; according to mythical tradition, she was a sea-nymph, whose lover Acis was killed by a rival suitor, the cyclops Polyphemus. The *dolce stil novo* was a poetic school which flourished in Italy in the thirteenth century. Initiated by the Bolognese Guido Guinizzelli (*c*.1235–*c*.75), its adherents included the Florentine poets Guido Cavalcanti (*c*.1260–1300), Cino da Pistoia (*c*.1270–*c*.1336) and Dante Alighieri (1265–1321).

20. Probably a reference to a common name for the heroine of a Gothic or historical novel.

21. Oh! Oh! I am all flourishing.

22. Come, come, may you come lest you make me die. (The second two lines are a nonsense refrain.)

23. Franz von Suppè (1819–95) was an Austrian composer of operettas.

24. '*Soli eravamo e senz'alcun sospetto.*' (Dante, *Inferno* V.129.) These are the words of Francesca da Rimini (see note 25 below).

25. Francesca da Rimini (*c*.1260–*c*.1285), daughter of Guido da Polenta (d.1310). Her 'sweet sin' was the sin of adultery: Francesca was put to death by her husband, Lanciotto (or Gianciotto) Malatesta, after being caught committing adultery with his brother Paolo.

26. A reference to an episode from Book III of *Gargantua and Pantagruel* (Books I–IV, 1532–52; Book V, 1562–4), by François Rabelais (*c.*1494–1553).

27. 'I will go in unto the altar of God. Unto God who gives joy to my youth.'

28. 'I shall bear witness to you, on the harp, God, my God!'

29. 'Glory be to the Father, and to the Son, and to the Holy Spirit.'

30. 'Lord, hear my prayer.'

31. 'We pray to you, Lord, through the merits of your saints.'

32. 'You alone are the Lord, you alone are the Most High, Jesus Christ.'

33. 'Lord have mercy. Christ have mercy. Lord have mercy.'

34. 'Holy Mary, pray for us!'

35. 'Virgin most prudent. Virgin most venerable. Virgin most praiseworthy.'

36. 'Mystical Rose. Tower of David. Tower of Ivory.'

37. 'Comforter of the afflicted, pray for us.'

38. 'Queen of virgins, Queen of all saints, pray for us!'

39. 'Pray for us, Holy Mother of God!'

Gabriele D'Annunzio was born Gaetano Rapagnetta in Pescara in 1863, the son of a wealthy farmer. He was educated in Prato and at the age of sixteen, his first work, *Primo vere*, a collection of poems, was published. D'Annunzio went on to study philology in Rome, but did not complete his studies, dedicating himself instead to journalism and writing. He wrote a number of poems in the early 1880s, which brought him wide acclaim, including '*Canto novo*' ['New Song'] (1882).

In 1883 D'Annunzio was married to the Duchess Maria Altemps Hardouin, though the marriage met with opposition from her family. The couple moved to Rome with their young son, Mario, in 1884, and D'Annunzio began to work on the journal *Tribuna*. He frequently attended the fashionable salons in Rome, and was strongly influenced by the aestheticism of contemporary European literature. His first novel *Il Piacere* [*The Child of Pleasure*] (1889) demonstrated this sophisticated sensualism. A number of other novels followed, including *Le Vergini delle Rocce* [*The Maidens of the Rock*] (1896), which showed the first influence of Friedrich Nietzsche in D'Annunzio's writing. His subsequent literature took on a visionary, nationalistic form and was much imitated by his contemporaries.

In 1891 the marriage to Hardouin had disintegrated, and three years later, D'Annunzio began a much talked-of affair with the actress Eleonora Duse, a relationship that inspired many of his plays, including *La Gioconda* (1899) and *Francesca da Rimini* (1901). D'Annunzio's public life was superficially that of a dandy, but, unlike his literary peers, he took an active interest in politics, and between 1898 and 1900 he served as a member of the Conservatives in the Italian parliament. In 1915, D'Annunzio was an outspoken advocate of Italy's entry into the war, in which he served as a fighter pilot.

D'Annunzio was dissatisfied with the post-war settlement, however, and with a group of volunteers, invaded and annexed the city of Fiume (now Rijeka in Croatia). The Government opposed his action but was unable to counteract his great public popularity, and D'Annunzio effectively held the town until he was forced to retreat in 1920. In 1922 D'Annunzio supported the Fascist coup, and was a close associate of

Benito Mussolini, though he took no part in the march on Rome and held no public post in the new government. His writing continued into the 1930s, and in 1937 he was made a president of the Italian Royal Academy. By this time, however, D'Annunzio was too ill to take on any of the responsibilities of the post, and early the following year he suffered a fatal stroke at his desk.

J.G. Nichols is a poet and translator. His published translations include the poems of Guido Gozzano (for which he was awarded the John Florio Prize), Giacomo Leopardi, and Petrarch (for which he won the Monselice Prize). He has also translated prose works by Ugo Foscolo, Giovanni Boccaccio, Giacomo Leopardi, Leonardo da Vinci, Luigi Pirandello, Giacomo Casanova, Giovanni Verga and Dante Alighieri, all published by Hesperus Press.

HESPERUS PRESS – 100 PAGES

Hesperus Press, as suggested by the Latin motto, is committed to bringing near what is far – far both in space and time. Works written by the greatest authors, and unjustly neglected or simply little known in the English-speaking world, are made accessible through new translations and a completely fresh editorial approach. Through these short classic works, each around 100 pages in length, the reader will be introduced to the greatest writers from all times and all cultures.

For more information on Hesperus Press, please visit our website: **www.hesperuspress.com**

ET REMOTISSIMA PROPE

SELECTED TITLES FROM HESPERUS PRESS

Gustave Flaubert *Memoirs of a Madman*

Alexander Pope *Scriblerus*

Ugo Foscolo *Last Letters of Jacopo Ortis*

Anton Chekhov *The Story of a Nobody*

Joseph von Eichendorff *Life of a Good-for-nothing*

Mark Twain *The Diary of Adam and Eve*

Giovanni Boccaccio *Life of Dante*

Victor Hugo *The Last Day of a Condemned Man*

Joseph Conrad *Heart of Darkness*

Edgar Allan Poe *Eureka*

Emile Zola *For a Night of Love*

Daniel Defoe *The King of Pirates*

Giacomo Leopardi *Thoughts*

Nikolai Gogol *The Squabble*

Franz Kafka *Metamorphosis*

Herman Melville *The Enchanted Isles*

Leonardo da Vinci *Prophecies*

Charles Baudelaire *On Wine and Hashish*

William Makepeace Thackeray *Rebecca and Rowena*

Wilkie Collins *Who Killed Zebedee?*

Théophile Gautier *The Jinx*

Charles Dickens *The Haunted House*

Luigi Pirandello *Loveless Love*

Fyodor Dostoevsky *Poor People*

E.T.A. Hoffmann *Mademoiselle de Scudéri*

Henry James *In the Cage*

Francis Petrarch *My Secret Book*

André Gide *Theseus*

D.H. Lawrence *The Fox*

Percy Bysshe Shelley *Zastrozzi*

Marquis de Sade *Incest*

Oscar Wilde *The Portrait of Mr W.H.*

Giacomo Casanova *The Duel*

Leo Tolstoy *Hadji Murat*

Friedrich von Schiller *The Ghost-seer*
Nathaniel Hawthorne *Rappaccini's Daughter*
Pietro Aretino *The School of Whoredom*
Honoré de Balzac *Colonel Chabert*
Thomas Hardy *Fellow-Townsmen*
Arthur Conan Doyle *The Tragedy of the Korosko*
Stendhal *Memoirs of an Egotist*
Katherine Mansfield *In a German Pension*
Giovanni Verga *Life in the Country*
Ivan Turgenev *Faust*
Theodor Storm *The Lake of the Bees*
F. Scott Fitzgerald *The Rich Boy*
Dante Alighieri *New Life*
Guy de Maupassant *Butterball*
Charlotte Brontë *The Green Dwarf*
Elizabeth Gaskell *Lois the Witch*
Joris-Karl Huysmans *With the Flow*
George Eliot *Amos Barton*
Alexander Pushkin *Dubrovsky*
Heinrich von Kleist *The Marquise of O–*